What People are Saying About
Mark's New Book, *A Simple Choice*

"This is Mark at his very best! Read and re-read this book. As a result, you'll be a better person at home, at work and in the community."
— Ron Smith, author of *HVAC Spells Wealth*

"The story of *A Simple Choice* is that all of one's problems are from within, but the wonderful answer is that all of one's solutions come from within also. You will realize that life is about other people, not about self."
— Don M. Green, executive director, Napoleon Hill Foundation

"Well-written and inspiring."
— Gary Weidner, editor, *Cleaner Times* magazine

"*A Simple Choice* is a collection of life parables inside a larger parable. The lessons taught will be lessons learned, memorable by their presentation and notable by their truth and power. When I read this book, I thought of many conversations I've had with Mark Matteson, one of the top motivators, speakers, and business coaches in the country. Reading *A Simple Choice* is like having Mark by your shoulder, coaching. You'll want to read it more than once. You'll want to take notes as you go. You'll want to buy copies for family and friends. This book can change your life."

— Matt Michel, CEO and president, The Service Roundtable

"We too rarely look at our lives as a series of choices. Mark's book, like the best of parables, reads more like a spontaneous gift. *A Simple Choice* points the way, plainly and beautifully. This book is worth savoring, which is a simple choice you'll be glad you made."
—Adams Hudson, consultant, speaker, author

"This book will help your soul sing. *A Simple Choice* will put a spring in your step and nudge you into asking yourself: How is my life going? *A Simple Choice* just might make it move more smoothly."
—Tom Peric, president, Galileo Communications

"*A Simple Choice* is a book for those who want to get the most out of themselves every single day and go to bed anxious for tomorrow. It takes work, it takes sacrifice, it takes guts, but it starts with attitude. Mark lays out the steps in an easy-to-follow path and he does it through an especially likeable character in Franklin. Savvy business people will use this book as a primer for their company's 'university' and then reap (and *share*) the great results which will follow."
—Mary Kellenberger, Nehlsen Communications

"Mark is the unique combination of business consulting, HVAC-specific knowledge, and gifted storyteller and writer. Add his message of inspiration. *A Simple Choice* is a special piece of work."
—Carol Fey, author and speaker

"Awesome!"
—Swen Nater, NBA player, coach

"*A Simple Choice* takes many of us down some familiar paths and reminds us of the importance and the value in bouncing back, of being true to our beliefs, and of being a giver, not a taker."
> —Dan O'Hara, senior vice president, National HVAC Service

"I found it very enjoyable and extremely motivating. A must read if you are in sales or manage salespeople."
> —George Athens, senior manager, TD Industries

"This book carries a powerful message that everyone needs to hear. This story will hit home, whatever your lot in life. I need to read it again."
> —Bill Baltzersen, director of corporate training, Temperature Equipment Corporation

"The book *A Simple Choice* is another example of how Mark is able to teach people life and business lessons while telling a great story. This is a great book and I recommend it to anyone who wants to grow a great business."
> —Allan Shero, president, Entek Corporation

"Mark has great insight into the human condition and a unique ability to translate those insights into real life lessons. *A Simple Choice* should be required reading for anyone who wants to be successful in business or in life."
> —Chuck Orton, president, MM Comfort Systems

"This is Mark's best book yet! Mark has a special way of showing how your business life and your personal life are connected to each other. The 'lessons learned' are applicable to everyone. I highly recommend this book for anyone in business and in need of that inspirational boost we all need occasionally. If you don't take away at least one way to improve your business or your personal life after reading this, you need to re-read it. I am very proud to know Mark and consider him one of the great coaches in my life."
> —Charlie Wallace, executive director, Quality Service Contractors

"Mark's book reminds us that happiness and success are not a right, but rather *A Simple Choice* rooted in the chosen, conscientious, caring, and compassionate service of others."
> —Drew Cameron, president, HVACSellutions.com.

"This story will whisper to you throughout your day and provide inspiration to be a steward to serve the higher good, while being successful and profitable in business and life. It allows us to find true balance and focus on what really matters. It reminds us that we are all in the 'service' business, no matter what industry we work in."
> —Fred Kahn, comfort24-7.com

"*A Simple Choice* is a beautiful story of not only surviving the impact of life changing events, but also growing through the changes; an example of the positive effects that transpire from people we meet in life. They arrive when we are least expecting them, but seemingly when we need them the most; another extraordinary best-seller for Mark Matteson!"
> —Tammy Divis, Department of Social and Health Services, WA State

"We are all mere students in the classroom of life; our lesson plans include love, hope, faith and charity. We learn from each other and our mistakes; passing grades leave room for improvement; when we fail we must repeat the course. Mark's book shows you how to get straight A's!"

—Dorothy Reddy, executive director, New York State PHCC

"I love this book and each character you bring into the story with Michael and Franklin. I look forward to getting my hands on several cases when it is published and giving this book to everyone I know."

—Michael Etchison, real estate entrepreneur

"WOW! *A Simple Choice* is amazing! Easy to read and loaded with insights into real life and business. I will get copies for my team."

—Colette Milar, sales manager, Milani Plumbing & Heating, Burnaby, British Columbia, Canada

"Mark is a gifted storyteller and has the remarkable ability to create a connection with the reader."

—Kristen Brown, manager, Northwest Natural Gas, Portland, OR

A SIMPLE CHOICE

A Fable of Redemption, Change & Hope

A SIMPLE CHOICE

Published by
Tremendous Life Books
206 West Allen Street
Mechanicsburg, PA 17055

Copyright © 2010 by Mark Matteson

ISBN: 978-1-933715-81-0

Printed in the United States of America

A SIMPLE CHOICE

A Fable of Redemption, Change & Hope

By Mark Matteson

Acknowledgements

My deepest gratitude to my mentor, publisher and friend, the late Charlie "Tremendous" Jones and to my extended family at Executive Books: Gloria Jones, Tracey Jones, Jason Liller, Greg Dixon, Pam Velencia, Candy Crawford, John Langel, for tolerating me with all my shortcomings. God's not done with me yet. Thanks for your patience with me. You are the richest kind of blessing in my life.

To my clients, too numerable to mention, you teach me more each time I work with you. Thank you for the opportunity to be a part of your work and personal life.

A special thanks to all my friends who contributed to this project: Debbie Matteson, my best friend for 29 years; my editor, Julie Taylor; and my valued colleagues Bill Bartmann, Dan Holohan, Gina Ippolito, Ron Smith, Matt Michel, Adams Hudson, Swen Nater, Kristen Brown, Ron Green, Alan Shero, Bill Baltzerson, George Athens, Tom Peric, Chuck Orton, Charlie, Wallace, Fred Kahn, Tammy Divis, John Woods, Michael Eitchison, Dorothy Reddy, Sam Wray, Dale Taylor, Drew Cameron,Gary Weidner, Collette Milar, Carol Fey, Mary Kellenberger, Marty Indursky, Andy Fracica, Tom Piscitelli, Your feedback and advice was timely, selfless and invaluable. Thank you.

Finally, to anyone who has ever suffered unexpected, tragic, and intense loss in your life, may you learn to go from Victim to Victor. Perhaps this book will assist you in that painful path. Enjoy the journey; the best is yet to come.

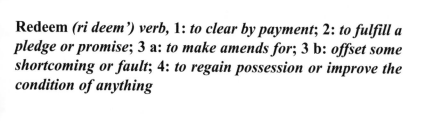

Redeem *(ri deem')* verb, **1**: *to clear by payment*; **2**: *to fulfill a pledge or promise*; **3 a**: *to make amends for*; **3 b**: *offset some shortcoming or fault*; **4**: *to regain possession or improve the condition of anything*

Table of Contents

Introduction by Tracey Jones

Life is all about *A Simple Choice.*

A great deal has been written about Servant Leadership and the transformational power it has on all aspects of a person's life. The influence of a Servant Leader can put you back on the path of finding true happiness and deliver a life of goal-driven successes.

However, this book takes it a step further. It beautifully portrays how this journey is not truly complete until you have dedicated your life to doing the same for others. Everyone can find elements of their own personal losses and struggles in the story of Mike Johnson, and his path to redemption is truly inspiring.

This story contains a tremendous amount of ideas on how to grow a thriving business. After completing the book, however, the reader will leave with so much more. They will possess the understanding and sense of purpose that the true Simple Choice is not only about helping ourselves, but in becoming a Servant Leader to others. *A Simple Choice* is all about Life.

Tracey Jones

Chapter 1

The Phone Call

It was November 19, 1998. I sat in the empty office with my father's old Colt .45. Was it the answer to my pain? It was a loaded pistol and it was staring at me across the desk, waiting for me to take action. *Do I really have the nerve to do it?*

When I was younger, I can remember saying that anyone who takes his own life is a coward. Ernest Hemingway took the easy way out. He wasn't man enough to face his problems. My self-pity had reached its zenith; I had never been so low. This was the loneliest place I had ever been, a black hole. At the worst of it, I no longer wanted to live, but I wasn't cowardly enough to take my own life. I felt evicted from life.

In the silence of twilight, the weather matched my mood: cold, gray, drizzling rain on that March day in Seattle. Did I have a choice? It was simple. I had to do it.

The phone, the bane of my existence, startled me out of my chair. I let it ring. The answering service would get it. It's what I pay them to do, by God. It kept ringing. By the tenth ring, I couldn't stand it. I've been conditioned to answer the phone. I'm in the service business and that's how people tell me they need my help. But I didn't feel like helping anyone. I was the one who needed help like never before in my life.

By the thirteenth ring, it was clear the service wasn't going to answer it. This had happened before, but never with this answering service. Ironically, as a cost-cutting measure, I had just recently switched back to the service I first used when I started this lousy business.

I picked up the phone, "Johnson Air." My tone reflected my mood, like a man with nothing to live for. I knew it and didn't care.

A kind voice on the other end said, "Sorry to bother you on a Saturday. We have water leaking from the ceiling and it's flooding the office. I removed the ceiling panel; it appears to be coming from the air-conditioning unit. Would it be at all possible to send a service technician out to the Smith Building on Third Avenue? It really is an emergency." The caller was very proper, well-spoken, and kind.

There was something in his voice, an authentic tone that made me want to help him. I shifted gears and went into trouble-shooting mode, a world I had lived in for more than 10 years as an air-conditioning serviceman.

"Do you know where the main water supply is for the building?" I asked, as a doctor in an emergency room might say to the EMT who had brought in the gunshot victim.

"No, and believe me, I looked."

"Okay, I'll be out there in about five minutes. Here's what I would like you to do while I'm en route. Go outside and look for a plate on the ground; they're usually in front of the building."

"You mean like the gas meter in front of a house, that kind of plate?" he asked.

"Exactly. Bring a wrench with you. The valve might not have a handle, just a little lever. It's a gate- or ball-valve. When you find it, turn it to the right and you'll hear the water flow slowing down. Call me on my cell phone if you don't find it." I gave him the number.

"Thank you!" he said. "And I am sorry, but I forgot to ask your name."

"Mike. Mike Johnson," I said.

"Thanks, Mister Mike, I'll get right on finding that valve!"

He must have been in his early 60s. He wore a pair of worn, blue bib overalls. He had on an old straw hat, the kind you see in old movies or at the state fair, except his was really worn, with holes at the corners, weather-beaten, and yet with just a touch of class.

He was mopping up the water with firm and even stokes, whirling the mop about like an artist with a great brush. The warehouse was attached to a beautiful office building. In the air was the pleasing aroma of a recently lit cigar. He set the mop against the wall and extended his hand. He had a firm handshake that took me by surprise.

"Franklin, Franklin Robinson," he said with a broad smile. "A distinct pleasure to meet you, Mister Mike, and I cannot thank you enough!"

"You found the shut-off valve," I said.

"Yes, thanks to your wisdom," he said. "It was in the front of the building and I didn't need the wrench. The valve had a big red handle. Yes, that did the trick. It stopped the water immediately."

It had been years since I worked with the tools, but like riding a bike, I knew just what to do. I went right to work. I isolated the water-cooled heat pump and repaired the leak in the ceiling. As I turned the water back on, Franklin said, "Voila!"

I put the tools away and felt a real sense of accomplishment, of being needed and wanted. It was an old feeling, one I hadn't felt for a very long time, one of being useful.

"What do we owe you?" Franklin asked in that same warm tone I had first heard on the phone.

"I'm not even going to write it up. This one is on the house," I said.

"Are you certain you want to do that? This company can certainly afford it. It's Saturday! I took several hours out of your precious day off. A young man like you would have normally been at a soccer or baseball game watching your kids play."

I think the pain on my face must have been obvious. Family. "No, not a big deal," I said. "I'm just glad we got the water shut off."

"There must be something I can do," Franklin said. He was watching me like a father watches a troubled child.

"No, Franklin, but thanks." I began to walk away, but then I turned back and said, "You know, on second thought, if you want to give my card to your boss, I'll follow up with a phone call on Monday. I did notice the filters were plugged solid with dirt and the coils could use a good cleaning. You could really use a building tune-up, a kind of one-time-maintenance."

I struggled to smile. I had unexpectedly fallen into my sales mode—just going through the motions. It really is like tying your shoes. Once you learn, you never forget. I've sold hundreds of service agreements with this strategy. "Who makes the decisions for the building?"

"That would be Steve Blackburn, our CFO. I'll give him your card and suggest he call you."

"I'll give him a call on Monday, Frank. Thanks. Do you prefer Frank or Franklin?" Considering my frame of mind just hours before, I was surprising myself. This man was bringing out the best in me.

"Thank you for asking. My friends call me Franklin."

"Have a good weekend, Franklin," I said. I could tell he knew something was wrong with me, something in my voice.

As I drove away, I realized he had pulled me back toward center. He got me out of myself long enough to remember why I do what I do and how much fun I used to have in this business. But it didn't really change my circumstances, did it?

Still, there was something about how this whole thing unfolded that didn't add up. Why did my phone ring? Why hadn't the answering service picked up the call? Why did I volunteer to go on this call? Something in his voice?

It seemed strange that he had the valve turned off and everything cleaned up so quickly. It was as if he knew where the valve was the whole time. Strange.

I drove back to my office, turned on the lights, and dropped the card on my desk with a yellow sticky note attached to it; a reminder to call Steve on Monday at 7:00 A.M. That's when CFOs are in the office with no secretary or receptionist to screen their calls; another sales insight, learned through years of trial and error.

And there was the pistol. It shocked me to see it sitting there, loaded. What had I been thinking? I opened the chamber, emptied the bullets, and threw them in the trash. I put the gun in my desk drawer and locked it.

How close I had come to ending my life.

Franklin had just saved my life. How could I ever thank him?

Chapter 2

The Leaf Spring

The next morning I woke up in a very different place, 180 degrees from the day before. Why? Was it Franklin? What had he done?

I called Steve Blackburn at precisely 6:59 on Monday morning. He answered his own phone and we set the appointment for Thursday at 2:00 P.M. He was grateful and ended our conversation with, "I'm really looking forward to meeting you. Thank you for all you did on Saturday, Mike. We should have the building cleaned up. I'll call this restoration company you recommended. This place really is a mess. We should have it somewhat presentable by then, you think?"

"Yes, Greg is an old friend and he does great work. He is a magician. You won't believe how quickly he'll have things back to normal. Greg is one of the few guys I still stay in touch with. I would trust him with . . ." I started to say "my kids." Has it really been a year?

"Mike? Are you still there?"

"Yes, sorry! I'm still here. You're more than welcome. We'll see you on Thursday at two o'clock."

The meeting with Steve flowed like water. I asked the key sales question, "If I could provide the service you deserve and lower your operating costs by ten percent, would you give us a chance for a year?" Steve paused for a moment and then said, "Of course, I would. It makes good business sense."

The deal was done, a $25,000 full-coverage agreement for three years. I had forgotten how much I love sales, the thrill of the hunt. I'm a good salesman. It has always been easy for me. I closed the deal in just three days.

As I went over "What went well?" and "What could I improve about the sale?" on paper, a habit I had acquired after attending a sales seminar, an odd thought struck me. In the three visits I had made to the Smith Building, I never saw Franklin. His name had never come up. Was he on vacation? I was disappointed. I was hoping to see him and thank him one last time. I decided to write a note to him instead:

Dear Franklin,

Thank you for the introduction to Steve. I am happy to report he chose to go forward with the service agreement. I am grateful to you for your kind referral. When time permits, perhaps we could have coffee or lunch, my treat. Hope to see you soon.

Mike Johnson

My mother taught me to write thank-you notes. Years later, I read in a sales book that an aspiring sales person should write a note of thanks after each visit to a client.

Four days later, the note came back marked, "Return to Sender." I hoped one day I would have the opportunity to thank Franklin in person and for more than just the business he had brought me.

The following week, it was time for my annual retreat to Lake Chelan. This was one of those family traditions that my wife had always insisted upon. My attitude the first time we went, ten years ago, was one of "contempt prior to investigation." In my ignorance at 24 years old, I did not understand that Lake Chelan is paradise. The largest lake in Washington State, fed by glacier water and too deep to measure, it's God's country (I figure it's His summer place anyway). The water is so clean you can drink it, so cold you can hardly stand it. But when the temperature outside is 98 degrees, jumping in the lake is a glorious contrast.

My kids used to be giddy during the few days leading up to the trip. God, I miss them terribly. Karen, too. It's just not fair. Why them? Why us? Why me? Why a drunk driver with a suspended license? Karen and the boys never knew what hit them that rainy night. This guy was going the wrong way on the freeway. His name was Roy Parker.

At 38, he had racked up 12 vehicle-related offenses, seven of them collisions. This was his first with fatalities. He walked away without a scratch. According to the state patrol's report, they found 14 empty beer bottles and another open one in his car. He said he had been on his way to the store for more. He served a short jail term. I lost my two precious boys and my wife of 12 years and he walked. It wasn't fair.

I get headaches when I think about it. Repeated visits to the doctor have been useless. Grief counseling has been a waste of time. None of these people understand what I go through each day. Not one of them understands. I suppose they mean well. "So sorry to hear about your family," or "What a tragedy, you're in our prayers." If I hear that one again, I'll lose it for sure.

This past year has felt like ten; I go in and out of phases. Some days the pain inside my heart feels like a vise, closing ever so slowly.

As I headed east, I was in one of my black moods, a reflective, one-man pity party. I was driving my new Dodge Ram truck, pulling my father-in-law's old 1968 camping trailer. It was quite a sight, like a broken-down old guy with a beautiful young woman at his side. But I couldn't get the lights to work on the new trailer we had bought. If I was going to Chelan, I had no choice but to take the old camper.

So I was going with this beat up old trailer, the one we had taken the kids camping in when they were infants. I'd changed many a diaper stooping in that old rattletrap. I'm about six-foot-five and the ceiling in that trailer is six-foot-two!

It was early Sunday morning when I got started on the four-hour drive. The Doobie Brothers were playing on the CD player, "Oh black water, keep on rolling, Mississippi moon won't you keep on shining on me."

BANG! It sounded like a 12-gauge shotgun. The trailer had locked up. I looked in the rear-view mirror and I could see the trailer had jack-knifed. Fortunately, no one else was on the road, but it was clear the trailer wasn't going anywhere. I climbed out of the truck and trudged back to see what was wrong. It appeared as if part of the frame or axle had pushed its way up into the floorboards. I couldn't tell exactly what was wrong but it looked bad. *Great, just what I need. What a way to start my vacation.* I grabbed my cell phone and called AAA.

The dispatcher said help would arrive in 30 minutes or less. Hope. The service business is about hope and peace of mind. That's what I had sold Steve Blackburn on the week before, hope. I felt better knowing someone was on the way. In the midst of the tempest, there was calm.

The driver was a stocky, bearded fellow with a broad smile and a disarming personality. His attitude was reassuring. His T-shirt was two sizes too small and his faded denim jeans were pushed down well below his generous belly. His shirt had one word: *Nirvana*. I smiled. He was a middle age version of one of those three guys. I tried not to look. He towed the trailer just a mile down the road to a parking lot in a little whistle-stop known as Perrinville. It's not even a town, just a stop sign and four corners. There was a little grocery store, a dentist's office, a veterinary clinic, a ceramics shop, and my friend Bill's office supply business. I signed the invoice and he wished me good luck. Right! I remember thinking, "If it wasn't for bad luck, I wouldn't have any luck at all. Can things get any worse? The tide is all the way out! When is it ever going to turn?"

A SIMPLE CHOICE

"Looks like quite a pickle you're in, young fella!" That voice! Could it be? I looked up. It was Franklin Robinson, complete with straw hat, blue bib overalls, cigar, and his million-dollar smile.

"Franklin, is that you?"

"Why yes indeed, Mister Mike! I saw you stranded and thought I could return the favor. Let's take a look at your trailer."

Without another word, he was under the trailer and mumbling, "Uh-huh, I see. Yes, that's quite a pickle."

Pickle? *No one I know, at least no one my age, ever uses that word.*

"Leaf spring. Yes sir, you've got a broken leaf spring. You know, I'll bet my friend has one in his shop. I'll be right back." He hopped in his 1952 Ford pickup and sped off before I could utter a word. Twenty minutes later, he was back with a rusty, weathered leaf spring in his hand. A leaf spring is a stack of metal strips, each about a quarter-inch thick and 18 inches long, banded together to provide support to the frame. What was almost magical was that if I were to call ten trailer shops in the region, I don't think that anyone would have this part in stock. The manufacturer stopped making that trailer 20 years ago. I would normally have to wait six weeks for delivery, but in less than two hours, Franklin had the new leaf spring installed. "Done!" he said.

"Franklin, how can I ever thank you? First the kind referral which resulted in a big sale and now this."

"My sincere pleasure, Mister Mike."

I knew how he felt, it was the helper's high. "What do I owe you, kind sir?" I asked.

"Oh, let's see; parts, labor, travel, tax, the total comes to… zilch, nada, nichts, nothing," he said with a splendid grin.

"Now look," I said, "you pull that old leaf spring out of thin air like David Copperfield, you invest hours of your Sunday morning . . ." I stopped, realizing that he was doing to me what I had done to him a few weeks earlier. I smiled. What could I say? "Let me at least buy you lunch or dinner. Fair enough?"

"Fair enough," he agreed.

At that moment, I thought to myself, "Does he want to sell me a twenty-five thousand dollar full-coverage maintenance agreement? I surely would buy it."

"I do have one favor to ask, though," Franklin said. "Actually, better make that two."

"Anything," I said.

"When you get ready to sell that beautiful old trailer, would you call me first?"

That was it? That's all he wants out of this deal? Who is this guy?

"Yes, of course. You'll have the right of first refusal. What's the second favor?" I asked.

"Do you know anybody that's looking for a parts driver, a deliveryman? That's my specialty!"

"Wait a minute Franklin; I thought you worked for Steve at the Smith Building."

"Used to, but it wasn't a good fit. They didn't need what I'm best at." His voice trailed off as if to say, don't ask anymore, it's personal.

"I'll be back from Lake Chelan in ten days. Come by our office on the twenty-second and we'll talk. I know a great place for lunch and we'll kill two birds with one stone. I'm looking for someone to fill just that position. The young guy we had went back to school, so this is perfect." I handed him my business card.

"Looking forward to it, Mister Mike, thank you. Have a safe trip to Chelan." Franklin sounded a little like a state trooper who lets you off with a warning.

"I will," I said, "I think I'll get a room at Campbell's Lodge and just drive the truck over, sans trailer."

This trip will be just what I need.

Chapter 3

The Parts Man

Iplugged the Doobie Brothers back in and was grooving on the soulful sounds of Michael McDonald's voice when the music stopped. The strange noise coming from the CD player sounded like a muffled pencil being ground in an old sharpener. *Oh, no! Not the CD player, not my music...* The disc was gone, mangled by a player well past its useful life. I tried ejecting it, no luck. Now I had no radio or CD player. Now what? *If it wasn't for bad luck . . .*

As I drove the four hours to Chelan without music, I had lots of time to think. It had been a long time since I had engaged in any real thinking. I had made a habit of avoiding thinking or feeling ever since the accident, but now I began to reflect on my past. It all seemed like a dream. You know the feeling, when you wake up from a good dream, not wanting it to end, dying to get back to it. Try as you might, falling asleep again never puts you back in the exact same place. That's how I felt as I returned to a place 18 months ago. I had a family, a loving wife and two boys, ages eight and twelve. Business was good, 30 employees and growing like crazy.

How had I gotten there? I'd like to believe my story is unique, but it's probably not. It had all started because I was sick and tired of making money for someone else and had decided to start my own company. I had been a salesman, working nearly 70 hours a week. Salespeople often hear things like, "You're always working 24/7. Everyone's a prospect." I nearly killed myself working and it had a negative impact on my family. Don't get me wrong, I love selling; I was born for it, like a fish to water or a squirrel to nuts.

Some of my friends thought I was nuts. While they dated, skied, and golfed, I wrote up proposals and put together presentations. I loved the thrill of the hunt. I loved the fact that there was no limit on my learning; therefore, there was no limit on my earnings. Once I figured that out, it was exhilarating. I was juiced. Selling, like sports, is subject to the laws of cause and effect, the unfailing boomerang, the law of sowing and reaping.

My father used to just shake his head. "Mister Extra-Mile," he called me. "Doggone it, Mikey; I never coached anyone quite like you. First one in the gym, last one to leave. I might change your name to 'Just-One-More-Shot' Johnson. I admire your ambition, son, but you gotta have balance." My dad coached me in basketball for eight years. He gave up a lot of his free time many a night in an old junior high school gym with my schoolmates and me. Man, what a team we had.

For eight years we played together, counting school games, over 100 games of basketball a year! It was heartbreaking to lose at the buzzer in the state championship game. It was as, through sales, I could make up for not winning it all back then.

My father preached "the Gospel of Excellence." He had some very fixed opinions. Basketball was life. He studied the best coaches of the day: John Wooden, Red Auerbach, Red Holzman, Denny Crumm, Vince Lombardi, and Tom Landry. I never really knew who these guys were, but my dad would read biographies on their lives and take notes in his journal. He would read them to us at odd moments or at practice. He would say:

Basketball is a metaphor for life. He would hold up a flat ball and ask new guys on the team what they thought it was?

A SIMPLE CHOICE

It's a metaphor. Some day your basketball career will be over. For some of you, that may be within a year or two. For others, it may be after a successful career in college or beyond. But someday, your ball will not have any air in it. My job as a coach is to prepare you for when that day comes.

It's the extra-mile attitude that makes all the difference.

You don't ever lose, but sometimes the shot clock runs out on you.

Why set goals? For what the goal will make of you when you achieve it.

Make up your mind that you are going to have a good attitude for as long as you live—I have no use for a sour-faced man. Furthermore, you commit to working hard and to finishing what you start.

Work like you will live forever. Live like you will die tomorrow.

Score off a pass, not off a dribble.

Offense sells tickets, but three things win basketball games: rebounds, defense, and free throws.

I smiled as I reflected on my dad's philosophy. It's amazing how much his words made their way into my life and formed my own philosophy. I was amazed how much of his philosophy I could remember. Maybe lo*sing the CD player hadn't been such a bad thing after all.*

Occasionally, he would simplify his phrases. When he packed our lunches, he would include these index cards. I would read the cards as I ate my lunch:

Be quick, but don't hurry.

You wouldn't care quite so much about what others think of you if you only realized how little they did!

The quality of my life is proportionate to the quality of my relationships.

MARK MATTESON

As I drove to Chelan, these memories of my father's sports and life philosophies swirled in my head like the dust clouds in an Eastern Washington wheat field. Growing up in a house full of women, two older sisters and my mom, I could always talk to my dad about anything. I would just say, "Dad, would you rebound for me?" In the silence, he would wait patiently and then say, "Watcha' feelin' inside, Sport?" It would all come pouring out. When I was done, I always felt better. I miss my dad. He died from Alzheimer's when I was 30 years old, too young. I didn't shed a tear at his funeral, though. In retrospect, that seems strange.

I had not thought of him in years; he is still alive to me in his words, but it's not the same. I have his journals, his books, and all those old photographs. They are so much more valuable than anything else he left behind. I had forgotten how much I really learned from him. He used to say, "You don't miss your water 'til your well runs dry." I was missing the water.

I had left a really good job at Steve's Air Conditioning Service. I was the sales manager/general manager. I worked my way up from driving parts to earning over $100,000 a year by age 27. Not bad for an average Joe with only a year of college. It was a good company and I grew up in it. I had started at 16, driving parts. That had been my first job. I fell in love with the business from day one. I was pretty arrogant at 16, though. I went around telling people, "One day I'm gonna own this joint." The owner, Steve Cooper, would smile and say, "He's not kiddin', better be nice to him; just might happen."

Steve was my Little League baseball coach. He was the one who asked me after we lost the Little League regional finals in extra innings, "Whatcha gonna do this winter?" The game hadn't been over 45 minutes and he was asking me about something that was five months away? When you're 11 years old, five months may as well be five years.

"I dunno. I guess I'll just watch Gilligan's Island?" I said. Hey, we had just lost the big game! What else is an 11-year-old gangly first baseman going to say to the one guy he respects as much as his father? When this guy said "Jump!" we asked "How high?"

He was the one coach who first affirmed the "Mr. Extra-Mile" moniker. Little did he know the real reason I was always the first one there. I was terrified of being late and disappointing him. The very first practice I had with him as a coach, I was five minutes late. I had to run five laps. I hated running laps.

The other reason was I had to walk to practice. The other kids all got rides from their parents, or they rode their bikes. Not me, I walked. After that first day, I made sure I was 15 minutes early for every practice. I stayed late to help him put away the equipment. He gave my teammates and me nicknames. They were all affirmations, always positive: "Clutch," "Wheels," and "Big Stick."

The two men who had most influenced my beliefs were still alive in my memory and in my work philosophy. I missed them both. It would be nice to have a good coach in my life again.

Although I loved coming here, this visit gave me an overwhelming sense of sadness, or was it boredom, anger, or depression? Yes, all of the above. Solitude is not a lonely feeling. In the past, my solitude getaways were never lonely. A friend said to me once, "It's possible to be in a room full of people and feel lonely." I never knew what he meant until now.

I ordered a drink, a light beer. I hadn't had a drink in ten years. Alcohol in my family was a disease; I knew it and I didn't care. *It's only one drink. No harm in that.* Seven drinks later, I stumbled to my room and passed out on the bed.

I awoke with an overwhelming thirst and a horrible taste in my mouth. I felt like I had been stuffed with cotton. What an awful feeling.

Kids playing on the beach served as my alarm. I glanced at the room's clock radio, 1:30 P.M.! That couldn't be right. I called the front desk. "Good afternoon, Mr. Johnson. How can I help you?" She sounded so chipper.

"What time do you have?" I sounded like Marlon Brando in *The Godfather*.

"It's one thirty-two, sir."

"Thanks," I mumbled, my head pounding.

What am I doing? I have never slept the morning away. As I sat up, my head felt like it was splitting in two. I stumbled to the bathroom, found some aspirin, and hopped in the shower for a solid 15 minutes. *Why did I drink all those beers? What happened? I don't even remember coming back to my room. Never again.*

So much for my firm resolve. The next night I switched to margaritas. Two young women joined my table and that's what they were having. For the next seven days, I drank a countless number of margaritas, read two John Grisham novels, burned, peeled, burned again, and finally tanned. I walked the beach, swam occasionally, and mostly felt sorry for myself. I was sinking into a black hole and I knew it. With each day that went by, I felt worse and drank more. The margaritas were numbing the pain. Little did I know the cure would become the problem.

I woke up the next day with a strange feeling. I wasn't in my room at Campbell's. Where was I? The ceiling was an off-white color. The bed was killing my back!

By now, my body was adjusting to the hangovers, but Mr. Cotton Mouth was ever-present. I sat up and looked around. I was in the Chelan City Jail! What had I done?

I called for the sheriff. "Whatcha' need, young fella?" he said with disgust in his voice.

"What happened?" I whispered, knowing from experience that if I spoke too loudly, my head would start thumping like a jackhammer.

"Well, I reckon you oughta ask the good folks at Campbell's. You tore up the place pretty good. That woman you were with is trouble. I wouldn't want to have to pay for all the damage you did: broken chairs, busted tables, and that fella you punched out is considering pressing charges. You knocked out two of his teeth."

A fight! I haven't been in a fight since high school!

"What's going to happen?" I asked meekly.

"Well, you're gonna have to post bail and come back in a few weeks to face the judge. I suggest you call your attorney."

On the drive back to Seattle, I had plenty of time to think. I remembered a quote I had heard years ago, a Chinese proverb, "First the man takes a drink, and then the drink takes a drink, and finally the drink takes the man." Was that what was happening to me? I was really afraid for the first time. I was out of control, not able to stop, even though I wanted to.

There was another problem; I could only remember bits and pieces of the last seven days. What had happened to me? I was drowning my grief in alcohol. I was in a whirlpool, spinning downward at a rapid pace.

The alcoholic, I was to find out later, starts out like any social drinker. The difference is that he is caught in an undertow which inexorably leads beyond social drinking. The drinker thinks he is in control, but an invisible line has been crossed and the former social drinker has become harmfully dependent on alcohol.

I was blissfully unaware of what lay ahead. I was like a man speeding down a country road toward a bridge that's out. I was about to learn that the emotional, physical, financial, and spiritual costs of drinking the way I was drinking are catastrophic.

Chapter 4

The Spiral Downward

I happened to catch a glimpse of myself in the mirror before I stumbled out the door that morning. The mirror had become like a neighbor's barking dog, a major source of irritation and something I just wished would be silent. I had cut myself shaving; brown flakes of dried blood filled the crease between my cheek and earlobe. Ignoring it, I walked out the door to work. The midday sun was warm and high in the sky.

It was getting harder to come to work each day. Even though this was my business, I didn't seem to care. When I first started my business six years ago, I came in at 6:15 each morning, Monday through Saturday. Since returning from Chelan, I was arriving a little later each week: 6:45 A.M. became 7:15, and then 8:00, 8:45, 9:30. Now six long weeks later, it was a good day if I arrived before 10:30. Though my employees said nothing, I could see it in their eyes. Everyone knew Old Mikey was losing it.

They began to quit me. I had built this company up to 30 employees, $4,500,000 a year in revenue. I had 20 of the best service technicians in the state.

My bankers had been happy, gladly extending my credit line and taking me to lunch regularly. Now they were calling me, leaving nasty ultimatums. Creditors were lining up and past due notices in red ink were multiplying like so many rabbits in a warren.

My first mentor once said to me, "A business is either growing or it's dying, there is no in-between. When you're green you're growing, when you're ripe you rot!" I was rotting on the vine.

The last straw came when Ron Sanders, my very best technician, entered my office. He was the first guy I had hired all those years ago. I saw in him at the time a guy who makes up for a lack of technical competence with an abundance of charm and people skills. I could tell by the look on his face he was about to give me the bad news.

"Mike, you know how much I respect you," he said. "You're like a father to me and it's killing me to see you doing this to yourself."

"The others are afraid to say anything to you. You're the owner, the boss."

I interrupted, "Get to the point, Ron. We've known each other too long to mince words or waste time with a bunch of sentimental crap. You're leaving, aren't you, you traitor! Who are you going to work for?"

Did I really just say that to one of the best people I knew? He was one of my oldest friends! What was happening to me? I feel like a bad actor in a B-movie. I can't pretend anymore; this is killing me and I've known it for a while now. It's getting worse. People who care about me are leaving or trying to help. I can lick this thing. I'll quit tomorrow.

"Mike, that's not important. What's important is you get yourself together, man. Customers are complaining to me. They're leaving and what's worse is that all your best techs are gone. This company is just a shell of what it once was. I won't stay here and watch you kill yourself one bottle at a time." He handed me a brochure. "Look. This is your business; you can run it into the ground if you want to, and that's your choice. But if you don't clean yourself up, get and stay sober, you're gonna lose more than your business!"

My employees were as pine trees are to an avalanche. My obsession had covered this entire company in a blanket of despair, doubt, sadness, and fear.

The brochure was for a treatment center for addicts. It had a picture of an evergreen tree, with the top branches of the tree representing a bird flying away. It read, "Whispering Pines Manor." I threw it in an open drawer and glared at Ron like a western gunfighter in Dodge City.

"Mike, you have *a simple choice.* Live or die. You gotta decide." With that, he threw his keys on the desk, gave me a hug, and left.

"Fine, I don't need you. I don't need any of you." After the door closed, I broke down, weeping like a little kid who just skinned his knees. I was crying for my lost family, I was crying for a business that was dying, but mostly I was crying for myself. I knew Ron was right. I remembered the thought I had a few months ago. *I no longer wanted to drink and no longer wanted to be sober, either. Once again, I felt evicted from life, but this time it felt permanent. I remembered the pistol. Where are the bullets? I reached in the desk drawer, opened the box of bullets, and loaded one chamber. I would only need one bullet to get the job done. It's a simple choice.*

The phone rang, breaking my suicidal thoughts. I picked it up. I don't know why. Habit.

"Mister Mike, Franklin Robinson. So sorry it's taken so long to get back to you. I've been on the East Coast; an old friend had passed away. I am across the street; I'd like to go to lunch and take you up on that offer of yours. Do you mind if I swing by right now? I know you're busy, but it's important. I'd consider it a huge favor."

Who was this guy? Why does he always call or show up when I am at my lowest point?

Grudgingly, I agreed to meet. I put the gun back into the drawer, leaving it loaded for the afternoon. In my drunken stupor, any attempt at taking my own life would probably have been in vain anyway. I probably would have missed; just my luck. The appointment with my maker would have to wait for later.

I wiped away the tears, composed myself, and met Franklin in the lobby.

Chapter 5

The Resume

Franklin was his usual chipper self. He smiled and shook my hand and as he did, he looked me up and down. I had seen that look a lot lately. It's the "this-guy-looks-awful-like-death-warmed-over" look. He was right. I did look like I had one foot in the grave. And I knew what I felt like inside—a man who was "less than"—but I suddenly realized that Franklin *did* know what I was feeling. He never said so, but I could tell.

We went to my favorite Japanese place, Shin Ju. The food was the best in town. The price was right and they knew me. I was their best customer; I ate there at least twice a week. Lately though, the owner, Tatsuya, was worried. He had known me for six years. Like everyone else I was close to, he was concerned for my well-being. A touch on the shoulder, a kind word of encouragement, he was trying to help.

"So good to see you, Mike-san. Tea?" he asked. He knew what I was going to order: gyoza, California roll, and white rice. Same thing I always order.

"The usual, Tat. Franklin, can I order for you?"

"By all means, Mike, please. I wouldn't know where to start," he said. I had a feeling that he would know where to start, but he was being kind.

"We'll have the California roll, yakisoba with chicken, and

gyoza, and rice, Tat. Thanks." My voice and attitude were both weak. I hadn't eaten properly in weeks. My health was deteriorating.

Franklin slid something over to me. It was a resume, but unlike any I had ever seen before. I composed myself. This gentle old man was like my first boss; he inspired me to want to impress him. He commanded respect. He had an aura, a presence. I needed him and I think that because I did, my attitude and manner changed almost immediately. I sat up, reached across the table, and opened the package.

It was without a doubt the strangest resume I had ever read. "Human being" as major work experience? Who was this guy? It was printed on the nicest parchment paper I had ever seen. It was thick, at least four times thicker than any paper we used at the office. He had rolled it up with a gold ribbon. In my 20-some years in the business, this was a first:

Franklin Robinson, PO Box 1211, Concrete, WA, (425) 555-7777

Major Work Experience:
Human Being
Parts Delivery Person, 50 years

Education:
Ph.D., Lessons of Life University, 83 years

References:

1. **My dog, Socrates: "I love him. I have never missed a meal."**

2. **Department of Licensing, State of Washington:**

   "Franklin has enjoyed a spotless driving record for

over 68 years without a ticket or parking infraction in 49 states."

I found myself in a bind. I desperately needed a new parts driver and there was no line at the door for the position. It was a $12-an-hour position, with no benefits. The most I had ever allocated for the position was 30 hours.

So I explained all of this to Franklin, and he just smiled a Cheshire Cat grin. When I was done, he leaned forward and lowered his voice to a warm whisper, "Would you like me to start this week, or is next week better for you, Mister Mike?"

Without even thinking, I said, "Next week would be fine. Are you comfortable driving a single-axle, twenty-seven-foot flatbed, in addition to the delivery van we have?" He smiled again and said, "I have my combination license, and any truck is just fine." I stood up, shook his hand, and said, "Well then I'll see you next Monday morning at seven-thirty."

Franklin stood and put on his weather-beaten straw hat, which still looked as if it had been around since 1910. "It will be my great privilege to work with you, Mister Mike. This promises to be a wonderful opportunity for service. I am grateful for the opportunity. Thank you."

After Franklin left, I thought about how he and I met, first the service call and the water leak, and then just weeks after that, the leaf spring on the truck.

I went back to my office and sighed when I saw Ron's keys on the desk.

I reopened the parchment paper scroll and reread Franklin's resume, shaking my head. "Sixty-eight years of driving experience without a ticket." That means this guy was 83 years old. I must be nuts. He's older than my grandfather, R.F. Johnson, would have been if he were still alive.

What I couldn't get out of my mind, though, was that when he walked in, I guessed him to be about 60 years old. Why did I feel so good around this guy; so at ease? In my gut, I knew that hiring him had been a good decision, but logic dictated that I truly must have lost my mind. He was so old!

While I was thinking about my decision, Helen's voice came on the speakerphone, "Mike, your next appointment is here."

Chapter 6

Hitting Bottom

Things at work continued as they had over the previous few months. Creditors kept calling, customers kept leaving, and I could not stop drinking. By now I was coming in at 11:30 A.M., looking like someone right off skid row. I didn't care; I was past caring, and yet, how could I be an alcoholic? Was that what Ron was trying to tell me?

I remember my father taking us down to the soup kitchen on Thanksgiving Day to feed the homeless when I was 13 years old. He warned me, "Son, this is where some folks who drink end up. Stay away from booze; you just never know if you're predisposed to alcoholism. Most of these poor souls are afflicted with a disease, an allergy of an unusual sort." He always paused for effect. "The phenomenon of craving isn't limited to a class of people. Alcohol is no respecter of the socio-economic pyramid. It doesn't care who you are, or how much money you have. These allergic types can never safely use alcohol in any form at all."

Pausing again and taking a deep breath, he said, "Once having formed the habit and finding they cannot break it, once having lost their self-confidence and their reliance upon things human, their problems pile up on them and become astonishingly difficult to solve. So they drink. Many die, others go insane, and the fortunate few get sober. Alcoholism is a progressive illness that can never be cured but which, like some other diseases, *can* be arrested. What makes this disease so unique is that it represents a combination of a physical sensitivity to alcohol and a mental obsession with drinking which, regardless of consequences, cannot be broken by willpower alone."

He never actually told me he was an alcoholic, but there was always something unspoken. Meetings, there was always talk of meetings. My mother would say, "Do you need a meeting, honey?" I never understood that. Then there was the occasional chance meeting of someone my father knew. They would almost always say the same thing, "I've heard all about you." I never had a clue what that meant. I had assumed my dad just bragged about our sports achievements.

I picked up the brochure that Ron had left me. The words jumped out off the page:

"If you or someone you know or love needs help, give Whispering Pines Manor a call, toll-free."

Whispering Pines Manor, right. I started to throw the brochure in the trash, but something stopped me. I kept reading,

"To facilitate treatment for those affected by alcohol and drugs, Whispering Pines Manor is recognized by the community as a leader in creating comprehensive, effective solutions for addictive behaviors."

I was drawn to the words: "addictive behaviors," "effective solutions," "affected by alcohol." I was definitely "affected," all right. The last page had anonymous quotes from satisfied clients:

"Whispering Pines program opened my eyes to what I can be."

"I am able to cope a lot easier with life and people around me."

"I've tried drunk and I've tried sober. I like sober better."

I like sober better. I like sober better. The phrase kept ringing in my head with the clarity of a Sunday-morning church bell in a small New England town.

I became aware that Franklin was standing there. I could feel his eyes on me. I looked up and tossed the brochure in the open drawer.

I picked up an unpaid invoice from an angry creditor, pretending that was what I had really been doing. It had stamped in red ink across the letter, "This is your final notice!" When I realized what I had in my hand, I was more embarrassed than being caught reading a treatment center brochure. I was trembling uncontrollably. The only thing that would stop the shakes was a drink. I couldn't wait to get out of the office; there was a bottle of whiskey in my truck. I had only been in the office an hour and I wanted to "go to (liquid) lunch."

"What can I do for you, Franklin?" I said, my voice hoarse and dry.

"I wondered about these bottles of refrigerant," he said. "Your service manager isn't in today and I hate to bother you, but do they go around back or in the warehouse?"

I sat up, knowing I looked like hell, and tucked in my shirt, the same one I had worn yesterday. I had not really slept the night before, and for the first time, I came into the office without a shower or any real sleep. I could only imagine what I looked like. I avoided all mirrors. They were too unkind. Franklin looked younger than I did.

"Around back...is fine," I paused to try to fix my voice. Booze and cigarettes; I was up to two packs a day. Somehow, the cigarettes had taken the place of at least two of my daily meals. I had lost 30 pounds. "How are you liking your first week here, Franklin?" He smiled and said, "Just fine, Mister Mike. I am certain I can make a difference here. There are a lot of parts that need to be delivered. I am especially fond of the rush orders, you know, emergency situations." Something about the way he said "emergency situations." I felt as though he was talking about the state of my health, both financial and physical, rather than our customers.

"Mister Mike, do you have a minute?"

"Yes, but only a minute. I am swamped today. I'm late for an appointment." My appointment was at a tavern, my daily ritual.

"I had an uncle; he was my favorite uncle of all my father's brothers. He was the youngest. He was born in eighteen seventy-eight, in the midst of one of the biggest boons in American history. General Ulysses S. Grant was president and railroads were much like the Internet is today. He went to work for none other than Andrew Carnegie, the Bill Gates of his day. The Wee Scotsman, as he was called, the Steel King. Carnegie had started at the bottom, as a telegrapher, going to night school, taking accounting, reading great books on the weekends, and working ten to twelve hours each day. He ascended rapidly. He built one of the largest steel conglomerates in the world. The first, and most loyal, forty-two managers who worked for him all became millionaires. Charles Schwab was one of his peers. In fact, my Uncle Joseph was competing with Schwab for the presidency of the company, and most people assumed he would win and run the company for Andrew."

At first, I resented this little history lesson, but the way in which Franklin told the story made it riveting, compelling, fascinating. This guy was no ordinary truck driver.

"Then tragedy struck. His wife of five years died in childbirth. That sort of thing happened a lot back then. He also lost his baby son. This was especially terrible, because they had tried to have children for five years with no success. My uncle was the hardest-working, most driven man I have ever known. He had a gift for getting along with people. He really cared. He was a great salesman. Everyone loved him, but shortly after the funeral, he started to change. He began drinking to kill the pain. Grief can be a terrible thing for some men, Mister Mike. He slowly began drinking his life away. It took him three years to lose it all, and finally, in nineteen twenty-one, he died a painful and sad death, locked away in a sanitarium. Gone at thirty-eight years old! They say he looked sixty-eight years old at the end. My father told us that story dozens of times. He never got over the loss of his baby brother. Joseph was the gifted one. They say the brighter a flame burns, the faster it fades. Those final years for Joseph were like a candle in the wind."

I was numb. Franklin finally broke the silence by apologizing for taking up so much of my valuable time. "I know you have an appointment. I'll just put those bottles around back. Make it a great day, Mister Mike."

Why did he tell me *that* story? First Ron with the brochure, and now Franklin with this story. These were warnings. And let's not forget all the looks. People I have known for years were looking at me as though I had leprosy.

I reached across the desk with a trembling hand and dialed. It took me three tries to get it right.

"Whispering Pines Manor, how may I help you?"

Chapter 7

Climbing Out of Hell

I didn't look good in orange. I was wearing orange slippers, an orange surgeon's shirt with a single pocket, and orange pants. What a sight. Talk about feeling self-conscious.

I couldn't get over how bad the other five people looked at the detox center. Man, were *they* in bad shape. One thing was clear, though, I felt inside like they looked on the outside. There were four of us: a carpenter, an engineer, an electrical contractor, and me.

The electrician's name was Arty. He was 54 years old. His company was bigger than my little company. I had read about him occasionally in the local paper. He had a hundred employees; he was a ruthless businessman and a low bidder—all the things I despised about the construction side of the business. I thought he was my alter ego, the exact opposite of me in every way. I was to find out later that we were more alike than we were different, though—more than I ever could have imagined.

Detox lasted for four days. I learned from the counselors that detoxification is the metabolic process by which toxins are changed. The purging of poisons follows. It takes about 90 days for your body to be completely free of the effects of alcohol and the first week was a living hell. I experienced nausea, vomiting, headaches, body aches, every conceivable ache you could possibly imagine and a dozen more you can't if you've never gone through it. It's a little like trying to explain snow to someone from Mexico. You just want to die.

I knew from recent experience that one drink would make it all better, one sip for that matter. The physical description is called delirium tremens. It's an involuntary shaking of the body or limbs, a fit of trembling. It's the body screaming out for what it has been conditioned to receive, King Alcohol.

The counselors were very kind and understanding. The kitchen was open and I had some of the best food I had eaten in weeks.

By the fourth day, the agony of detox subsided and I never want to go through that again. I made arrangements to go through their rigorous outpatient program. Most of the people who work at Whispering Pines are recovering alcoholics. They know. They understand. They've been there.

Theresa started in the kitchen 15 years ago. She was now the administrator. *Had I sold her a maintenance agreement five years earlier?* Sure enough, while I was there, one of *our* service trucks pulled up out front! One of our few remaining technicians showed up for a service call to Whispering Pines! I recalled now that I had seen work orders come across my desk. Maybe that's why it had been comfortable for me to call; it was a familiar name. In my alcoholic stupor, the name didn't ring a bell. How strange is fate? I had ended up at one of my customer's facility.

Theresa made a point of visiting me. She was petite, kindly, compassionate, and bright-eyed. Her gentle streaks of gray hair gave away her true age of late 30s or early 40s. "Mike, I am glad you're here. I was especially pleased to hear you have enrolled in our treatment program. I just have one quick question about your insurance." She and I hit it off immediately. She was to become one of my closest friends. Before I left, I found a note on my bed. It was printed on flowery stationery that smelled like lilacs. I opened the note:

A SIMPLE CHOICE

Mike,
I know how hard this is for you. I was right where you are now fifteen years ago. Hang in there and trust the process. People who get sick with this disease can and do get well. We are here to help you get your train back on its track. I believe you will come out on the other side of this experience stronger, with longer legs for bigger strides.
Theresa W.

As I wiped tears from my eyes, feelings of gratitude come over me for the first time in more than a year. I had almost lost it all. I thought back to the revolver in my desk drawer and how close I had come to ending my own life, not once but twice. I thought about my family, lost to me. I thought about Ron giving me that brochure, and how hard it must have been for him to do that. I thought about other people for the first time in months. And I thought about Franklin.

"Mister Mike? So nice to see you! You look great! Do you have a minute?" *Did I have a minute? I had all day; it was Franklin, always so gracious, so kind. Was this guy a mind reader?* He stood in front of me with a contactor, a 30-amp, 3-pole, Allen-Bradley contactor. "I am here to deliver this part. Is Don around? He called me to deliver this part."

I felt embarrassed standing there on my last day of detox in my orange outfit. He immediately put me at ease. He had that effect on me. "I brought one other thing; I hope you don't mind."

He handed me a book, a beautiful leather-bound journal. It had a ribbon running through the center that served as a page marker. It was gorgeous. I knew enough about stationery to know this bound blank book cost at least ninety bucks. For him, that was half-a-week's wages. I took it in my hands and held it like a new baby. I caressed it as tears welled in my eyes.

"Franklin, you should not have done this. This is absolutely beautiful! Thank you, my friend," I said, holding back the other tears inside.

"You're quite welcome. I determined you might have some extra time on your hands for a while. I have found a journal allows me to quiet the clatter in my mind. In a way, you're on a retreat, though it will probably turn out to be an *advance*." His eyes twinkled when he said that. "From today on, things will only get better. You're right where you're supposed to be."

He paused, just as my father used to, and then he said, "Things are just fine at the office. Something amazing happened while you were gone, some good news I thought you would *appreciate*." He placed extra emphasis on the word appreciate, smiling broadly. "Ron has inexplicably returned. In fact, he is the one who asked me to deliver this part. Your service manager thought it would be okay to hire him back without your permission. Ron thought I should tell you he was back, and give you the opportunity to think about whether you want him to stay."

"That is just fine! I am delighted to have him back." Franklin nodded and smiled. "Franklin, I can't thank you enough for all you've done." He started to speak, but I held up my hand. "No, please let me finish. I would not be here if not for you and Ron. You guys saved my life, and more than once. When I get back next week, we'll talk some more. I am late for a mandatory meeting right now and it's *not* at a tavern. Thanks again."

Franklin touched my shoulder and said, "I look forward to our next conversation, Mister Mike. Enjoy the journal."

As I sat in the meeting, I did not hear a word anyone else said. I thought about the note from Theresa, the journal from Franklin, and Ron coming back. I began to cry. These were different tears from those of the past year. These were not tears of self-pity. They were tears of gratitude, the first I had shed since my first son was born.

Chapter 8

Reconstruction

As I sat in the first inpatient class, a fellow named Bob read this to us:

"Welcome. You are a patient in this two-year treatment because you are sick with a chronic addiction. It's a potentially fatal dependency on a chemical substance that interferes with your daily life. Because your condition is chronic, you cannot be cured. But you can be treated successfully.

"Our treatment has two objectives: to arrest your disease and to recover your person. While you are inpatient, you will be safely withdrawn from all alcohol and chemicals, treated for the immediate symptoms of your illness, and you will initiate your personal recovery. Upon discharge from this facility, you will continue treatment as an outpatient for two years. This is necessary to ensure full recovery and to minimize the chance of a relapse."

My mind drifted to the judge's sentence. He told me that the charges against me in Chelan had been dropped, provided I successfully complete my treatment. Two years deferred prosecution if...

I smiled to myself. If . . .

I refocused on what Bob was reading. *I'd better pay attention.*

"Rehabilitation—that is, organizing a new way of life with

new patterns of living and thinking—is your primary purpose in treatment. Upon satisfactory completion of inpatient treatment, you will be able to lead a normal life, free from chemicals, provided you embrace and continue the therapy offered to you as an outpatient.

"Your unreserved cooperation is essential to your recovery. Mere compliance, going through the motions without internal acceptance and personal motivation, will leave you sick." *He stared directly at me...*

"You will find the atmosphere here friendly and our personnel understanding of your condition and problems. You will gain much support from your fellow patients, and you will be able to contribute much toward their recovery as well, both during and after your residence here. Now please take a few minutes to read the handout you received at the beginning of class. The specific steps of our recovery program are outlined here. Think of it as your road map."

The one-page handout was concise and informative. It read:

The treatment is in phases:
Phase One = Observation and detox
Phase Two = Inpatient treatment
Phase Three = Outpatient treatment

We will use a combination of approaches:

Education
Through 54 lectures, various selected films, and prescribed readings, you will learn about the nature and dynamics of your progressive and chronic disease. You will discover the physical, social, and personal deterioration that accompany it.

Group Therapy
Repeated experiences in groups of people who suffer from

A SIMPLE CHOICE

the same affliction provide you with encounters designed to confront and break down defense mechanisms and negative attitudinal postures, which always accompany chemical addictions. Group therapy also enables you to recognize and accept who you are, and which specific attitudes and behavioral patterns must be modified in order to live comfortably with dependence on harmful chemicals.

I was in for a long journey.

The counselor was a confident and learned man, warm, open, and sincere. He had a strong presence. I noticed he always had a book with him. In the cafeteria, when I saw him for the first time, he was reading *Oliver Twist*, by Charles Dickens. I didn't speak to him then because he was obviously engrossed in the 19th-century slums of London, but during our first meeting, he told us many things. The one thing he said that really blew me away, though, was, "You might consider getting yourself a journal, a blank book. It doesn't have to be fancy, just an old-style, spiral bound notebook. You're going to find that it's a great way to quiet the clatter in your head."

Franklin! How did he know?

When I got home, I opened the journal to begin my page-a-day commitment to this new growth tool, MY journal. It made sense; my father kept one for most of his life, and Franklin had given me this for a reason. My counselor had strongly suggested using one. It all made sense, so I surrendered.

I turned the cover and on the inside cover page was this inscription from Franklin:

Mister Mike,

"No man is an island entire of itself. Each is a piece of the continent, a part of the main. If a clod be washed away by the sea, Europe is the less, as well as if a promontory were, as well as if a manor of thy own or thy friends' were. Each man's death diminishes me, because I am involved in

mankind; and therefore, send not to know for whom the bell tolls, it tolls for thee."

John Donne

John Donne was an English poet, prose writer, and clergyman. He was born in 1572 and died in 1631. In the small towns of seventeenth-century England, the church bell peeled whenever someone died. Most people would send a child to run and find out just who had died and how.

Mr. Donne's point in his poem was, "The bell is ringing for you! Don't waste any time! Don't worry about what others are doing; mind your own garden. At least, that is what I remember from high school English.

Funny, I don't remember a lot from high school, but I remember all of that as if it happened yesterday. I can thank a great teacher that I had for one year. He was my mentor and his name was Bruce Evans. He was my first high school basketball coach and the best coach the school ever had. He went on to coach girls' basketball and those girls went to state every year. He was humble, kind, and had a strong presence that comes from really knowing your stuff. He loved English and basketball.

The first journaling I did was during my English class. I am sure I don't have any of those old journals now, but I do have this new one from Franklin.

I opened the journal to the middle and wrote my first notes:

December 11, 1999 – Sunday 7:14 PM

The first entry into my new journal, huh, I am uncomfortable doing this and yet, it feels easier than I thought it would. There was a reason my dad kept one all these years. Now FR has come into my life. Why? No matter, I'm glad.

There is a little sign on the wall at Whispering Pines. It reads:

Admission

A SIMPLE CHOICE

Compliance
Defiant Dependence
Acceptance
Surrender

In-patient was really uncomfortable for me, but I wanted to be here. No, that's not true. I *hated* being here, every minute of it. It was asking for too much honesty, too much reality. I have been pushing my feelings of despair, resentment, fear, and anger down deep into myself for a very long time, for years even before the accident. But here I was. If. . .

We engaged in group discussions. People kept asking me, "How did that make you feel?" We wrote out our First Step.

We watched movies about alcohol and discussed them. There was the Hallmark production with James Woods as Bill Wilson, or Bill W., as he is known in AA circles. Most of it I couldn't relate to, except for wanting to stop drinking and to get my life back.

I wanted to stop! I wanted to stop the feelings of worthlessness and shame, of feeling lonely in a crowded room, of wondering why my insides didn't match everyone else's outside, of feeling "less than," of not liking myself much, of being so consumed with self-pity, it oozed from every pore, of knowing no one cares or understands.

During the third week, something strange happened. Someone told my story. No, I don't mean they actually told *my* story, I mean they told their story and it was me! It was like hearing a song that is new, one that you have never heard before, but because the lyrics strike a chord with you. It's a song you can relate to. I had made a connection to Arty, the electrician.

Arty had worked his way up from the ranks, just as I had. He started out driving parts. He moved up and became an electrician's helper, then to apprentice, and eventually a journeyman. A good electrician in New York City can make $120,000 a year. It's not quite that good in Seattle. Most guys are happy and content working for 30 years in the trades and then retiring secure and comfortable, but that wasn't for Arty, and it certainly wasn't for me.

Arty had played football in high school and achieved All State recognition. He earned a full scholarship to the University of Washington. He was a sturdy fellow, about six-two and 250 pounds, with sandy blond hair (at least what was left of it). He combed it back in a way that reminded me of Jack Warden, the character actor who always seems to play a football coach or a businessman in his movies. For Arty, college was short-lived once a knee injury ended his football-playing days.

He had been in the industry about 12 years when he struck out on his own. His story is similar to the stories of thousands of guys around this country who say to themselves, "I can do better than this guy I'm working for." That is exactly what I said when I left to start my company.

Arty had more than 100 electricians working for him. Our paths crossed a few times on large projects. His trucks were everywhere. As he told his story, I could feel his sense of pride that comes from building something unique, something worthwhile. It reminded me of the first really great thing I built in woodshop. I brought it home to my parents and I felt so proud. My mother acted as though I had built a cathedral.

Arty's partner embezzled most of the money in the business and left Arty holding the bag. Arty lost a major lawsuit in court, from some bad advice his attorney had given him, and before he knew it, he was in Chapter 13 Bankruptcy.

"It's an embarrassing process, and all so public," Arty said. "I felt so violated and so angry. People went bankrupt for many reasons: a health disaster, drug or alcohol addiction, or in my case, simple fraud."

As bad as I felt for Arty, I had some hopeful thoughts. *We have it pretty darn good in this country. I am struggling with my business, but I am not wiped out, and nor am I in bankruptcy. I sense Arty will rebuild someday, and he'll be stronger for this experience in the long run.* I hadn't quite yet made the connection that this could also be true for me. These were thoughts of gratitude and objectivity that I had not engaged in for more than a year. Things were starting to change for the good for me.

By listening to his story, I learned about Arty's descent into hell. I could relate. I could relate to his sense of loss, of anger and betrayal. His anger was toward a crooked partner, now long gone. He's probably in South America with three million in cash. My anger was directed toward a drunk driver and God. I had been going through my own brand of self-inflicted bankruptcy.

My next journal entry was short and sweet:

December 18, 1999
Resentment comes so easily to me. It's the common denominator of all alcoholics. I've got some work to do.

Resentment—it's the number-one reason alcoholics go back to drinking. Harboring RESENTMENT is like taking poison and expecting the other person to die!

I think the fog is starting to lift. I feel better each day. As I write this, I still think of Roy Parker and those old negative feelings well up inside me. What did they say in class? Oh yes, "Avoid criticism, argument, and resentment (C.A.R.). If you are resentful, go wash that person's car...the resentment always goes away."

The objective of recovery is to find a new way to live.

I must be rid of my RESENTMENTS and the ghosts that accompany them. Then find a way to keep them from coming back. But how?

Just before going to bed, I reached over on the nightstand, where I usually kept my special journal. It was becoming a good friend, a trusted listener.

I was more than a little surprised when I opened it. Franklin had made another entry on the fifth page of my journal:

Mister Mike,
If you are reading this, it probably means you are making progress and feel much better than you did when you were wearing orange slippers!

May this journal be a lighthouse for you in the fog of life.

Many a man has kept a diary, a log, a journal. For me, it has been a way to capture the events of the day, that is, life's lessons, for all time. It has afforded me the chance to get <u>from</u> the day, not just through it. May it add years to your life and life to your years!

Your friend always,
Franklin Robinson

P.S.
I am grateful that we met. I am proud to be your friend first, your employee second. Thank you for the opportunity to deliver important parts in the service call of life.

Chapter 9

Are You a Servant Leader?

The few remaining people who stayed at my company were incredibly kind to me when I returned. It was now mid-January; I had been away for more than six weeks. January is usually a busy time for us since it is the heating season. Business was picking up. Almost every person greeted me with a hearty handshake and sincere comments that I looked good. I know I felt better than I looked.

I had learned so much in the last two months. I felt like Jimmy Stewart in *It's a Wonderful Life*. I had a second chance, a new beginning, and a new lease on life. It occurred to me that I had a responsibility to the people who had stayed with me. I would change things for sure, but how? I had made sweeping changes in my personal and spiritual life, but my work life? This was another story. Where would I find the answers, the guidelines for changing my company and its culture?

There was a knock on the door. "Come in," I said.

"Mister Mike, I'm sorry to disturb you. I wanted to welcome you back. I'm proud of you."

"Thank you, Franklin," I said. He meant what he said. When Franklin spoke or praised, it felt like my father was talking to me again. It meant so much.

"You must feel even better than you look," he said.

"Yes," I said, "like a million bucks. Listen, Franklin, I want to thank you for all you have done for me. When I was in treatment, a lot of people told me that you really picked up the slack. You were in here at five-thirty in the morning, making coffee, cleaning up, getting things set up for the day, and some days you were delivering parts to our service guys well past six o'clock in the evening. Is that true?"

He hesitated for a moment, and said, "I lived in Florida for more than a year, when I was just a young guy. I suppose I was fifty-four or so. There was a devastating hurricane that year. Edith was her name.

"Everyone pitched in after Edith left. It was an amazing thing. Something happens in times of crisis; people pull together and they become one with a common purpose. They do it because they know it's the right thing to do, and they do it gladly. I was just a worker among workers. It was actually fun. I did it gladly. Hey, what else am I going to do with my time?"

"Nonetheless, I am grateful. I don't know what I would do without you," I said, holding back a tear.

"It is my sincere pleasure, Mister Mike. I am just glad to have you back. You look like a new man!"

"You're not really just a parts driver, are you, Franklin?" I said.

"No, Mister Mike. I'm more like the guy with the ugly dog. You see, there was this fellow with an incredibly ugly dog. That dog was so ugly, people would either make fun of it or look away in horror. Well, that never really bothered this fellow. He loved that dog. He loved him so much he entered this dog in every show that came along. Of course, the dog was so ugly he never won a prize. Finally, one day his best friend pulled him aside and challenged him. 'Why do you insist on taking this dog to shows where he will never win a prize!' 'I know,' said the fellow, 'but look at all the great dogs he has been able to associate with!' I am the ugly dog, but I'm grateful. I have been blessed to have associated with many a fine show dog!"

A SIMPLE CHOICE

I smiled. Franklin was so disarming, so humble. I knew he was much more than the "ugly dog."

"Mister Mike, I am just a parts driver, it's all I've ever really been. I deliver what people need, when they need it." He paused a moment and then said, "Sometimes, I deliver things people didn't order, and I provide what they don't expect."

"Like my journal?" I said.

Franklin smiled and nodded. "Yes. I try to make a difference in people's lives. Most people are operating in a kind of lock step. We are all capable of so much more. Latent potential exists in all of us. It lays dormant, waiting to be pulled to the surface. Only the tip of the iceberg shows."

"Franklin, I have to ask; you've been around, and you know far more than you let on. May I ask you some tough questions?"

"Fire away, Mister Mike," he said.

"I have come to some conclusions lately. I have had a lot of time to think during the past six weeks. I want to change some things around here and I would like your advice." I hesitated a moment. "Confidentially."

"I am all ears," he said.

"Before these things happened, before I lost my family, my health, and nearly my sanity, all I cared about was winning. Making money, winning jobs, that's what mattered. I had this blind passion to be the best, to win the championship that eluded me in sports so many years ago. I was able to accomplish a great deal, but then I hit a wall. It all cost too much, Franklin. I wasn't happy. I was half-empty. There must be a better way."

"You had a Pyrrhic victory, Mister Mike."

"A what?" I asked.

"A Pyrrhic victory. Pyrrhus was the king of Epirus, a district in ancient Greece. He was very ambitious and he expanded his territories by adding the western parts of the neighboring kingdoms of Macedonia and Thessaly. In two hundred eighty-one B.C.E., the people of Tarentum, a Greek colony in southern

Italy then at war with the Romans, requested the aid of Pyrrhus. Early in two hundred eighty B.C.E., he sailed for Tarentum with a force of twenty-five thousand men, and twenty elephants. He defeated the Romans at Heraclea, but aroused the ill will of the Greek people by his despotic attitude. He won the war but at a great cost to his army; hence the term Pyrrhic victory. *It means we paid too great a price for our victory.*"

"I do not want to win at all costs. I don't want to be like Pyrrhus," I said, shaking my head in recognition.

"Good, glad to hear that," Franklin said, "So you want to become a Servant Leader?"

"A what?"

"A Servant Leader. Simply put, that's a person who leads with his heart—a person who cares about people he's leading, and does the right thing from a human perspective." He smiled at me. "There is one catch, though, Mister Mike. You cannot, you *must* not, make this decision lightly. Once you grab hold of this philosophy, you will not be able to let go of it."

I nodded in understanding and he smiled again. "However, if you do embrace this new way of life, this unique, misunderstood, and often criticized path, it will fundamentally change everything about your life." He lowered his voice and said, "Could you be ready for such a bold leap of faith?"

"Yes!" I said, "I am." I felt like I was saying yes to a pastor at a marriage ceremony.

"Well, if I may be so bold, if you agree, you must trust me and agree to commit to this for one year with the open mind of a child. I will take you far out of your comfort zone. I will ask you to think and act in ways you may not like. You must be willing to *trust* me as you have never trusted anyone before. Is it a deal?" He held out his hand. I had never seen him look so serious.

"Deal!" I said, grabbing his hand.

"Good. I have a story for you now, Mister Mike."

"Saint Francis of Assisi was born in Italy in the year eleven

A SIMPLE CHOICE

hundred eighty-one. His father was a very successful cloth merchant and he wanted his son to follow him into the family business. His mother was devoutly religious and had aspirations for him to the clergy. As a young man, his commitment was to sport, music, French poetry, and money. In today's language, he only cared about the ballpark, bedroom, and billfold. As a soldier in his early twenties, he had a series of experiences that deeply affected him. First he had a dream which was so real that he saw it as a sign from God. The next experience was a chance meeting with a leper who was begging for alms. The suffering of this man so impacted Francis, he exchanged clothes with him and then begged for the rest of the day. Finally, he heard a sermon that clarified his life's purpose. He went to Rome and started a new order of monks, dedicated to serving the poor. He died in twelve hundred twenty-six, but not before leaving behind an extraordinary legacy and perhaps the greatest prayer ever written:

'Father, make me an instrument of your peace.
Where there is hatred, let me sow love,
Where there is injury, pardon,
Where there is doubt, faith,
Where there is despair, hope,
Where there is darkness, light and
Where there is sadness, joy.
Grant that I may not so much seek to be consoled as to console,
To be understood, as to understand;
To be loved as to love,
For it is in giving we receive;
It is in pardoning that we are pardoned;
It is in dying, that we are born to eternal life.'

"This prayer is profound in its simplicity, Mister Mike. It asks you do the opposite of what most people do. Each line is a declaration and a lifelong commitment to change. As we insinuate these simple requests into our daily routine, subtle shifts begin to occur. We realize life is about other people. It's not about self.

"If you want to understand Servant Leadership, read the book of Luke in the New Testament. When you are done, take some notes. We can talk about it afterward. Mister Mike, my point is we need to be mindful as leaders. Stewardship is the key. Leaders are really just trusted stewards. Let's talk more tomorrow. I've got some parts to deliver."

He had delivered enough parts to keep my head spinning all night. People are most important. Things will be different from now on. I wasn't sure how, but I was clear on the what-and-why!

Chapter 10

Appreciation, as Rain to Dry Flowers

Franklin and I agreed to meet for coffee every Wednesday at a Starbuck's in the University District. It was filled with college students toting textbooks. Every big city has a coffee shop like this one. It attracts people of all races, lifestyles, ages and socio-economic status. Two dominant themes exist there, coffee and learning. One table has an attractive young woman in her early twenties. She's wearing a dark-blue sweatshirt over a baby-blue blouse. It's one-size too small and it's exposing her navel ring button. Alongside her is an overstuffed chair and a tiny, three-legged table. There are nine law textbooks stacked high on the table. Next to the books is the most important object of all, her standard, college-ruled notebook. It's filled with chicken scratches, highlighter markings, and rough draft reports or dissertations. It's her journal of education.

The table next to her has a single novel, Tom Clancy's latest thriller. A middle-age man, slightly balding and thick in the waist, sits there. He is well-dressed. He's taking a break from the rat race, just long enough to lose himself in a good story. The soft jazz stylings of Chet Baker float in the air. *"Let's get lost, lost in each other's arms, let's get lost, let them send out alarms . . ."* This place had charm, ambiance, and college chic.

I was definitely the willing student. The professor had just walked in. Franklin always wore the same outfit: worn blue coveralls, clean, almost pressed, with his signature straw hat and unlit cigar. I noticed his shoes for the first time. They were a beautiful pair of brown, Red Wing work boots, the kind that go halfway up your calf. They were polished to a military shine.

Despite his country appearance, Franklin had a commanding presence. People stopped and stared. He flashed that smile and people smiled back. They knew him here. This was his place. He said hello to five people as he made his way to my table.

Each of those people was better for having seen him. They were like unlit candles before Franklin touched them with his light. The man was a bright flame in a dark room. Amazing.

"What did you just do? I watched each of those people change as you spoke to them. You have such a gift."

"Oh, I don't know about that," Franklin said. "They are all great people. What I do is very simple, Mister Mike." He leaned in and whispered, "Here is my little secret." He handed me a small index card with the word **Appreciation** written on one side. I turned it over and read, "Appreciation. To esteem, to prize, to value, to rate highly. (In financial terms, it means 'To raise the value of!')."

"Mister Mike, we are not talking about insincere flattery. Appreciation is not something mechanical, and it's not from the head. Sincere appreciation comes from the heart." He was smiling like the Chesire Cat in *Alice in Wonderland*.

"I remember my favorite coaches all did that," I said. "They would praise specific behavior, like hustling after a loose ball, or second effort."

"Exactly!" Franklin said, moving his hands in concert with his words, "It is an honest assessment of specific performance or effort. It is real, random, and repeated. It's from the heart and full of emotion and meaning. Make it soon, make it specific, and most of all, make it sincere."

A SIMPLE CHOICE

"So, people need praise," I said. "They hope for it, and if they don't receive it, they begin to fish for it, subtly or openly." I knew the question was really a statement, but I was hoping for his validation.

He smiled.

"The deepest craving in the human condition is the need to be appreciated. It is so important for each of us to feel valued by others. Here is the ironic part of praise…it's easy! It opens up conversation," Franklin said.

Lowering his voice to a whisper, as though sharing a high-level government secret, he said, "Here is a little test for you over the next week. I want you to catch people doing things well, and when you do, offer up real praise. Be specific. Be honest. Be sincere. And when YOU receive a compliment, pay attention to how it makes you feel. What do you do and say in response to praise? Pay attention. It's just a little test. Keep notes in your journal. Let me know what you learn. It's time for me to go, Mister Mike."

We walked out to his beautifully restored 1952 Ford pick-up and Socrates, his dog, began wagging his tail. He was a 12-year-old golden Labrador (84 in dog years), and he was Franklin's trusted Tonto. "Time for me to go, Mister Mike. I take old Socrates to the beach every day. It's *his* time now. Let's talk next week."

As he drove away in his old Ford, I had a warm feeling in my heart. It was the same feeling I first experienced when Steve Cooper patted me on the back after I hit a game-winning double in Little League. I was 11 years old then. It felt good to feel that way again.

It's strange. It's as if this guy had dropped down from heaven to become my mentor! He delivers parts for me! He is my employee! He doesn't appear to have much money, yet he is the most joyful person I have ever met. I feel sorry for him, and yet, there is something about him. I can't put my finger on it.

MARK MATTESON

March 24, 1999 – Sat.
Home Office – 7:10 PM

I praised Bill Thompson today for the project sales he closed. He was grateful; I could tell because his face just lit up. He smiled and said, "Thanks, Mike!" I thought he was going to cry! Wow! I just never knew! Helen, my receptionist, changed her hairstyle. I said it made her look younger (she is in her late 40s). She just beamed, and then started typing a proposal for me at record speed. What a difference a little praise makes. PRAISE PAYS!

"Praise is the grease on the wheels of business and of life." I must make a conscious effort to do it every day with all the people I come in contact with: suppliers, employees, customers, friends, and family!

Chapter 11

Respect, My Fair Lady

"You know, Mike, I am always amazed how little I really know, and I am constantly amazed at how stupid I was five years ago," Franklin said.

"That's why I use a dictionary every day to look up words I think I know. Here is what I'm working on this week." He handed me an index card that had the word **Respect** written on it. It read, "Respect" is defined as "To regard. To matter. Pay homage. To admire. To honor. To approve. To consider. To love."

"I didn't fully understand what that word meant until today, Mister Mike. I'm working on liking myself a little more today. Shoot, at eighty-four, I'd better like myself! I am going to be in this vessel until I go, so I may as well like me. You know something? I'm the kind of person I would like to spend the rest of my life with." He smiled and added, "I am so old that I don't even buy green bananas anymore!" He had that twinkle in his eye again. I laughed.

It felt good to laugh out loud. I hadn't done that for a long time. Never had much to laugh about, I reckon. This old guy makes me smile and he makes me laugh. He's always happy, always smiling. What's his story? Some day I'll find out.

Did you ever see *My Fair Lady*, Mister Mike?" Franklin

asked with that get-ready-to-learn-something tone in his voice.

"No. Wasn't that a musical? I think I've seen it at the video store."

"Yes, it was a musical, but it was more than that. It captured eleven Academy Awards in nineteen sixty-two, including Best Picture. It features many fine performances. I especially liked Rex Harrison, a famous British stage actor, playing the part of Professor Higgins, and Audrey Hepburn as Eliza Doolittle, the Cockney flower girl turned into a princess (on a bet). That is the premise. It was originally a play, a smash hit in London. It was one of the most successful plays George Bernard Shaw wrote. Mr. Shaw called his play *Pygmalion*. Pygmalion is in ancient Greek mythology. He was a sculptor who carved a statue of a beautiful woman. She was his ideal woman, and he fell in love with her. Venus, the goddess of love, took pity on Pygmalion and turned the statue into a living woman so that he could marry her.

"In the musical adaptation of Mr. Shaw's play, Colonel Pickering and Professor Higgins make a bet. Can Higgins, a speech teacher and technically competent coach, teach Eliza what she needs to become a lady?

"Could she be passed off as such at an important ball in six months? The game was on. They would clean her up, teach her how to walk, speak proper English, and be a lady. What neither man counted on, though, was that they would fall in love with Eliza.

"Near the end of the story, after Eliza has made an impressive impact on everyone she met at the ball, she ponders her future and the marriage offers that came pouring in.

"Analyzing what has happened to her in her personal transformation, she says to Colonel Pickering, *'The first day we met, you called me Miss Doolittle. That was the beginning of self-respect for me. There were a hundred little things you did for me that you did not notice. You see, they came naturally to you. I'm not blaming him* (and here, she meant Henry Higgins, who had not treated her so graciously), *it's his way, isn't it? But it made such a difference to me that you didn't do it* (treat her without respect). *You see, really and truly, apart from the things anyone can pick up* (clothes, the proper way of speaking, and so on), *the difference between a lady and a flower girl is not how she behaves, but how she is treated. I shall always be a flower girl to Professor Higgins, because he always treats me as a flower girl and always will; but I know I can be a lady to you, Colonel Pickering, because you always treat me as a lady, and always will.'"*

I was rocked by the truth in this. It was a blinding flash of the obvious. He was dead-on with his analogy. I knew it to be true from my own experience.

"Some managers always treat their subordinates in a way that leads to superior performance," Franklin said. "But most managers, like Professor Higgins, unintentionally treat their subordinates in a way that leads to lower performance than they are capable of performing. If managers understand and apply this great truth, the performance of the employees will be directly linked to the manager's expectations and how they are treated."

I could tell Franklin not only believed this with all his heart, he lived it. I had experienced a taste of it and it was like magic. I was writing notes as quickly as I could, punctuation and grammar be damned.

"Positive self-regard," Franklin said. "If the manager has positive self-regard, he seems to exert its force by creating in others a sense of confidence and high expectations, not unlike Colonel Pickering and Eliza Doolittle. Employees will try hard to meet his expectations and behave as they believe they are expected to behave."

Seeing that I was taking notes, he stopped talking. He was a considerate guy, reading the needs of others by listening to their body language. I aspired to that level of empathy.

In a moment, he continued. "A Pygmalion leader, a Servant

Leader, be he a coach, pastor, or a CEO, must acquire industry knowledge and job skills required to be confident of your high expectations. This will make him credible to his employees. As the leader, you must assume responsibility for your own growth and personal development. That is why I will often say, 'As the coach grows, so grows the team.'

"Bear Bryant was one of the most successful football coaches in college history. He had a habit of giving away all the credit for the wins and assuming all the responsibility for the losses. His players loved him for that. I try to remember that."

I was a little numb from all this information. Finally, I said, "I've got a lot of work to do."

He gave me that fatherly smile, from coach to player. He delivered the message and I received it loud and clear. He knew it and I knew it. It was a magical moment. He sat back, sipped his latte and said, "Your head is probably spinning, Mister Mike. Let's take a little break. If you have any questions, write them down and we'll go over them next week."

I rented *My Fair Lady* from the video store and was struck by the humanity of the beautiful story and the wonderful music. They don't make musicals like that any more!

April 6, 1999 – Car – Monday – 1:30 PM

"Treat people as they are, they remain. Treat them as they can be, they become!"

I want to be like Colonel Pickering, <u>NOT</u> like Professor Higgins!

Watch *My Fair Lady* again tonight!

One of the keys to changing other people's performance is to affirm a future positive picture of them—to them aloud—and to keep affirming it until they can see the changes themselves, praising the slightest progress along the way!

Chapter 12

Understanding–Give It Away First

Things had begun to turn around in a very short time. Technicians and customers began flocking back to my company like the swallows returning to Mission San Juan Capistrano in Southern California. Despite my hitting bottom on every level, what happened to me over the next year was nothing short of a miracle. I was beginning to feel a little like Job in the Old Testament.

Franklin and his dog Socrates were a big part of that. Franklin took Socrates everywhere. He was such a friendly dog, especially with kids. He always had a tennis ball in his mouth, patiently waiting for any willing participant to engage in a spirited game of fetch. "Labs are a very friendly breed," Franklin explained to me one day. "But Socrates is especially congenial. He loves people..." His voice trailed off as he reached into the top pocket of his overalls, the one by his heart. He handed me what had now become the much anticipated index card.

"Sounds like his master," I said with a smile.

I had begun taping the cards Franklin gave me into my journal. I dedicated at least five pages to each of these cards. As I came across articles, picked up ideas in conversation or observation, I added notes in my journal about the topic we focused on each week. I was building a body of information in my journal about "servant leadership."

The card read:

Understand *verb,* 1. To perceive the meaning of; grasp the idea of; comprehend. 2. To be thoroughly familiar with; apprehend clearly the character, nature, or subtleties of.

Understanding *noun,* 1. The mental process of one who comprehends. 2. Superior powers of discernment, a skill in dealing with or handling something.

As I read this card, I thought about how fortunate I was to have found Franklin (or had Franklin found me). I had read about angels once in a magazine article; I think it was the *Atlantic Monthly.* Franklin was one-part angel and one-part business professor.

The professor interrupted my train of thought.

"Mister Mike, that's kind of you to say that, but I believe it's truly the other way around. Socrates has taught me a great deal about people and life. Socrates is an odd name for a dog, I know, but you see, Socrates was a very wise man, a great philosopher, who lived in Athens, Greece between four hundred sixty-nine and three hundred ninety-nine B.C.E. He had the nickname of the 'Gadfly of Athens'. He used questions to develop latent ideas to force people to question outdated beliefs or elicit admissions from an opponent in an effort to change people's thinking. He was so good at forcing people to think, the nobility of his day felt threatened. He was way ahead of his time and it ultimately cost him his life. My dog is just like that. You see, the first year I had him he was just 'Boy'." The dog's ears perked up when he heard that word.

"He's getting on in years now. He will soon be in his nineties. He and I have much in common. He can get through to more people with that tennis ball and relentless tail wagging than I ever could on my best day. He has helped more people than I have. Dogs appreciate others. Dogs understand others. Dogs respect others. They do it automatically, especially Labs, and in particular this amazing hound. He was the runt of the litter, the last one to go. His mother was killed by a car two days after he was born. You see, Mister Mike, he is a survivor. Perhaps that is why he and I make such a good team." He cut himself off, hesitating to explain himself any further right now.

That just left me more curious than before about Franklin's past. "He is your Tonto, eh, Kemosabe?" I said with a grin. Franklin appeared somewhat startled, like when you remember someone's name that you haven't seen for 20 years, and yet they don't remember you.

"You are more right than you know, Mister Mike."

I picked up the ball and threw it. Socrates jogged off after like a very enthusiastic 90-year-old. We went about 20 rounds and I finally gave in. I think he might have gladly gone 20 more rounds with me, had I been willing. It was impossible not to like this dog, or his master.

"Isn't it amazing how dogs are always glad to see you? They're so loyal," I said.

"Man's best friend," Franklin said quickly. "He is my best friend, aren't you, boy!" Franklin rubbed Socrates' ears, and the old dog rewarded him with a shimmy wag. "Dogs accept us unconditionally. They intuitively know and understand our moods and they give us exactly what we need when we need it. They have a sixth sense about this." He smiled. "It is understanding that gives us the ability to have peace. When we understand the other fellow's point of view, and he understands ours, then we can sit down and work out differences."

I told Franklin about an article I read in a business magazine the previous week. "The CEO of Domino's Pizza, in his first week on the job, hired what he called the 'Executive VP of People First', and began searching for keys to enhance his employees' performance. Based on an eighty-percent response to a company-wide survey, enhanced employee programs are being rolled out to keep people involved and committed to the company's success. Every business strategy issue is being reviewed to see what effect each has on the company's people."

"You're impressed with the CEO's approach," Frankly asked softly.

"Yes!" I said. "I think it is so cool he cares that much. The article ended with an amazing statistic. The last company this CEO led had a turnover of less than ten percent. That's what I want. I want people to stay with me and love coming to work each day.

"But how do leaders such as this stay in touch with what's going on with the people?" I asked. "The bigger my company became, the more removed I felt from the new people my service manager was hiring. I didn't even know the first names of the last ten people he hired without looking at their shirts!"

"Ah, the challenges of leadership and growth," Franklin said. "I can only tell you what I have observed other companies doing. One large contractor with more than one hundred employees took pictures of each person and hung the photos, along with each person's name, in the hallway."

I grabbed my journal and began taking notes. *I have been acting as if Franklin will be around forever, I thought. I had better capture every insight this guy offers. He is, after all, 83 years old. How much longer will he be around?*

"Another way is to conduct surveys," he said.

"Surveys? What sort of surveys and to whom?"

"A fine question indeed," Franklin said. "A Servant Leader recognizes two sets of customers: internal, his employees; and external, his customers. The most enlightened leaders talk to both sets of customers regularly. They stay close. They use focus groups and anonymously written, or face-to-face, surveys."

"You think I should bring in a consultant?" I asked.

"Do you trust me?" he said.

"Yes, but you're different. You work for me. It's not the same."

"Your father coached you for a long time in sports, did he not?" Franklin knew the answer to the question before I answered it.

I nodded. "Yes."

"Did you ever come home from practice with some profound bit of new knowledge, some exciting new insight you just learned from a coach that you couldn't wait to share with your dad?"

"Sure; almost every week, once I got serious about improving."

"Your father was probably just as excited about your new insight as you were. I would go as far as to say he put those coaches in your path at different times, as a different voice, one other than his own."

"Now that I think about it, yes he did," I said.

"It's the same principle. Some consultants can be very helpful. Just be sure there is a beginning, a middle, and an end, with some clearly-defined results in between."

"Dogs don't need to conduct annual surveys; they are always reading our body language and extra-verbal tones. Since they only understand the meaning of a few words, they rely on what they see in our gestures, and hear in the tone, volume, and pace of our voice. They intuitively know what to do, based on what they see and hear," Franklin said.

"Like when they creep up and put their head on our laps at just the right moment, precisely when we need to be comforted?" I said.

"Exactly!" Franklin said. I could tell from his tone and body language that he was pleased. I was starting to understand. It made me feel good to please him. I was learning so much.

"General Robert E. Lee was a native Virginian and he was

faithful to the South right up until the day he died. The War of the States, as he called it, was a bitter pill for him to swallow."

I would come to enjoy Franklin's personal stories best. They had a special appeal, an extra emotional emphasis that made them special.

"General Robert E. Lee was a great leader, perhaps the finest general on both sides of the war. President Lincoln knew that. Because of General Lee's great skill and strategic decision making, he enjoyed the upper hand in battle after battle with the Northern generals. President Lincoln went through one bad leader after another until he finally found Ulysses S. Grant.

"General Lee was forced to make a difficult decision early on in the war. When Virginia seceded from the union, he was forced to pledge his allegiance to the South, a war he knew in his heart they could not win. Nevertheless, Lee gave it his all – more for Virginia than for the collective South. General Lee had empathy, self- and mutual respect, dignity, education, charisma, and an uncanny ability to understand the human condition.

"In addition to all of his other positive qualities, he also possessed chivalry. On one occasion, he sent Jefferson Davis a captured letter that had been written by a Union soldier. The letter described the demoralization of the Union army because of General McClellan's indecision, poor leadership, and ultimate retreat. 'I would suggest that no publicity be given the name of the writer of this letter, as it would injure him, without materially benefiting us,' General Lee wrote."

"He preserved the dignity of the Union soldier when it would have been so easy to do the opposite," I said.

"Yes," Franklin nodded. "That's right. He thought of others. At Gettysburg, he passed a wounded Union soldier, who seeing Lee, raised himself up and shouted in defiance, 'Hurrah for the North!' The soldier later reported, 'The general heard me, looked, stopped his horse, dismounted, and came towards me. I confess that at first I thought he meant to kill me. But as he came up, he looked down at me with such a sad expression upon his face, that all fear left me, and I wondered what he was about. He extended his hand to me, and grasping mine firmly and looking right into my eyes, he said, 'My son, I hope you will soon be well.'"

"Franklin, that is amazing. I am not sure I could do that."

"He was an extraordinary man. After a decisive victory at Chancellorsville, General Lee gave his first attention to the wounded on both sides. While he was thus engaged, a note arrived from Stonewall Jackson, congratulating him on his victory. 'Say to General Jackson,' General Lee replied, 'the victory is his, and the congratulations are due to him!'"

Slowing down a little, he finished his stories about Lee with the best one of all.

"After the disaster at Gettysburg, when General Wilcox came forward and lamented the state of his brigade, General Lee took him by the hand and said, 'Never mind, General. All this has been my fault; it is I who lost this fight, and you must help me out of it the best way you can.'"

Franklin's stories had a profound effect on me. They were easy to remember, and they always had at least one point that was meaningful.

I want to become a great storyteller!

April 16, 1999

Remember the lessons from dogs. Pay attention to where someone is. Are they sad? Are they happy? Are they frustrated? Dogs understand and adjust accordingly.

General Lee was loyal. He gave credit away when it was clearly due him. He accepted responsibility for failure when it was obviously not his fault. He had huge amounts of empathy for others, even his country's enemies.

Chapter 13

Human Potential Released

Ron Sanders came into my office with a curious look on his face and an odd tone in his voice. "Do you have a minute, Mike?"

"I always have time for you, Ron," I said. "How is your family?"

"Fine, Mike, thanks. Joey hit a homer last night on majors. Did I tell you he has two teams on majors fighting over him?" he asked proudly. "It's really ironic. When he didn't make majors, I was really upset. Out of pure frustration, I called a friend who is a coach at the majors level, and asked him what my options were. I was really whining to him. He's an old friend and very understanding. After we talked, I concluded that what I could do was work with Joey up at the field, helping him get bigger than his job. I pitched to him, caught him pitching, and hit grounders to him four times a week for a month. That's what I *could* do. While we were spending all of that one-on-one time, I took the time to affirm what a natural he was, and how proud I was of him. I told him he would dominate on first farm. He is a big kid for ten years old."

I listened intently. I could tell Ron appreciated that I had first asked him about his family and that he appreciated even more that I listened intently to what he had to say. Listening to people had become my new hobby. As with anything else, I was getting better with practice. "It sounds like the Serenity Prayer in action," I said.

"Exactly!" Ron said, smiling.

Reinhold Niebuhr was a born in 1892. He was an American theologian and philosopher. Twelve-step programs all around the world have adopted an abridged version of Niebuhr's now-famous prayer. He wrote, "God, grant me the serenity to accept the things I cannot change, the courage to change the things I can, and the wisdom to know the difference."

I had come to rely on that prayer. A psychiatrist friend once told me that applying that simple prayer on a daily basis was the best thing to do for good mental management. The heart of this prayer is the practice of *acceptance* first, and positive *action* second. He went on to say, "We don't see things as they are. We see things as *we* are."

"You focused on what you could do and let the rest go." I said to Ron. He was beaming now. He knew that I had been attending some of the same AA meetings he was attending, and a few he didn't know about. It was working. I had asked some-one I respected to be my sponsor and I was now working the 12 Steps of AA. It felt as if someone had lifted a great weight off my shoulders.

"It's always fun to talk sports with you, Mike. You've made huge strides in just a few months. I am proud of you, buddy, for having the courage to get and stay sober after everything that's happened to you." Ron's pride was obvious. After all, he had skin in the game.

"I've got to ask you, where did you find that Franklin fella? He is amazing. He says the most poignant things and at just the right time. I feel so confident and sure of myself when I am around him."

"Me too," I said, echoing his sentiment.

"Keep hiring guys like him and we'll own the market," Ron said.

"Thanks, Ron, I feel the same way. Franklin listens well, doesn't he?"

"He sure does!" Ron said. "More than that, he observes other people's needs and emotions and he delivers just what is needed. I'm talking about more than just parts, Mike."

"I know just what you mean. He seems to bring out the best in people; he certainly has in me. He always seems to have just the *right part* at the right time."

Sensing I was busy, Ron got up to leave. "I just had to let you know, Mike. Keep up the great work."

I smiled. *I loved having Ron back. How thankful I am to be alive.*

"Oh, before I forget, I have a lead for you." He handed me a form we had created, all filled out with the prospect's signature at the bottom. "This guy needs a full-coverage maintenance agreement. He's ready to go. Give him a call and go close the deal, will ya'? It's a nice building. Brand-new DDC controls, great people, just the kind of building our younger technicians will love to work in." This was the fourth solid lead Ron had given me this month. I had closed the previous three with ease. With all these solid leads, Ron made selling easy for me.

It had only been two months since I implemented the leads program. I got the idea, the "ah-ha" moment, after Franklin told me a story about another mechanical contractor he knew in Michigan.

It's a simple plan. When a technician meets a new customer who obviously needs regular maintenance, the technician hands the prospect a form to fill out. The prospect fills it out and signs it, simple, easy. We've had a 90-percent close ratio on signed lead forms. I handed out movie tickets and dinner coupons as a spiff. Everybody wins. Some companies use cold hard cash; I prefer the "take-your-wife-out-on-the-company" approach.

A SIMPLE CHOICE

Ron had always had a way with people. His interpersonal skills were top-notch. He would make a great salesman. He was almost 40, and he was ready for what I was about to propose to him.

"Thanks Ron, I will follow up on this right away. Keep up the good work!"

Ron smiled as he walked out of my office. He looked like he felt nine feet tall. "Praise pays," Franklin had said to me one day. Ron appreciated the compliment. He knew it was real.

Perhaps it's time to promote Ron to a sales position. "Promote from within." Where had I heard that?

The phone rang, interrupting my thoughts. "Mikey, you old dog, how are you, pal?" It was Arty, the electrician from Whispering Pines, my treatment buddy.

"I'm doing great!" I said. "I'm on this side of the grass and grateful! How are you, my friend?"

"Great! Business is booming. Do you have a few minutes?" he asked and I was a bit taken back by his empathy. Arty is such a hard-charging guy.

"I always have time for you. What's up?"

"You remember that dirty, rotten former partner of mine? The one who ran off with my bank account? I told you about him when we were in treatment."

"Your former bookkeeper and partner," I said.

"Yeah. They found him in Caracas, Venezuela! He's been deported back to the States. Apparently, he burned the wrong guys down there and the Feds found him. Can you believe it?"

"What about the three million dollars?" I asked, a little embarrassed immediately after asking. After all, it was none of my business.

"That's why I called," Arty said, putting me at ease. "There's two million five-hundred thousand dollars left! It's frozen right now, but I will eventually have access to it. But here's the weird part, Mikey. My sponsor had been on me for months to pray for this guy, something I was loathe to do."

"Page five hundred fifty-two…" I said, reading his thoughts.

"Exactly!" he said. "I hated that guy for a long time. Huge resentment. It drove me to drink. But then I prayed for him every day for more than three weeks. You know, I prayed that his life would be blessed; that he would be happy and have peace. Can you imagine that? He is sitting in the Seattle jail even as we speak, awaiting trial."

"I'm really happy for you, Arty. What's next?"

"That's the strange part. I don't care about the money. It represents my old life. Don't get me wrong, I care about profit, just not THAT money. Does that make any sense or have I lost my marbles?"

I knew exactly what he meant. It was symbolic. It was almost as though keeping any part of the old life would be hypocrisy. This was indeed a miracle. Arty, as I had found out in treatment, was more driven and focused on profit than I had been.

"My business is booming," he said. "I started a service business to complement the construction side. I have ten guys doing just service! I don't care about the money. I have a crazy idea and I wanted to run it by someone who understands. That's why I called you."

"What can I do?" I asked, feeling a little uneasy, not sure what he was going to say next.

"Well, it's just an idea for now. What would you say to starting a halfway house? You know; a place for guys to go who have been in jail, are getting out of treatment and want or need to be rehabilitated, a place to stay for six months. I don't expect to make any money on this. If we break even that would be fine. You know, non-profit. I want to put *that* money to good use; I sure don't want it. It represents my old life. I feel like it should go toward helping guys like you and me who don't have the opportunities you and I are blessed with. Hey look, it's just a thought. Percolate on it a while and get back to me."

A SIMPLE CHOICE

"It's an interesting idea," I said, uncertain of the role I could play in all of this. "I'll give it some thought."

"Hey, old buddy, I gotta go. I'll call you next week. We've been doing some work in a building you guys used to work in. I told the owner how well you were doing. He wants to talk with you again. You remember Steve Blackburn?"

I smiled. "Yep, I sure do. Nice guy."

"Listen, we'll have lunch with him next week. Look at your calendar and let me know which day is best, Wednesday or Friday. Take care, old buddy, and remember, page five hundred fifty-two."

"Arty?" I said. "One last question."

"Shoot!" he said.

"Didn't you tell me in treatment that you promote from within? With your electricians, I mean."

"Whenever we can," he said. "Probably ninety-five percent of the time. Most of my guys don't leave when they know they have a career path. They usually talk to me first before they consider hanging up the tools. This usually happens when they're in their late-thirties or early-forties. I would think it would be the same for you." He paused a moment and then said, "It's one of the few things I did right. I think of it as man-ifesting the potential of my guys. It's sort of like releasing the emergency brake on the car. The car always goes faster and gets better gas mileage when the brake is off," he laughed.

It's so simple. Steve did that for me. It makes so much sense. Okay, I have just created a new policy.

"Oh, Mikey, one last thing. Can I tell you a story that I read recently?"

"Sure!" *Suddenly everyone in my life is a storyteller.* I grinned.

"A certain shopkeeper sent his son to learn about the secret of happiness from the wisest man in the world. He traveled the entire day to reach the wise man's castle, which was deep in the Black Forest of Germany. The young man was asked to wait, as many people had come to seek wisdom. Several hours passed before the young man heard his name called. As he entered the wise man's private office, he was struck by the simplicity of the furnishings. The castle was resplendent with the finest tapestries, artwork, statues, and ornate furniture. Humbled by the great man's age, flowing white hair, and beard, he asked for the secret of happiness. The wise man handed him a spoon full of precious oil. 'Walk around my castle for the next hour with this spoon of oil. Be mindful to retain every drop. Come back in exactly sixty minutes for an accounting.'

"The young man walked for an hour and didn't spill a single drop of the oil. Proudly, he returned to the wise man. 'You can see that I was successful in keeping the oil in the spoon,' he said. The wise man smiled and said, 'As you walked, did you notice my fine collection of tapestries? It is the finest collection in the whole world.' The young man replied, 'No, I was busy minding the oil.' There was a deep sadness in his voice. 'Then walk again,' the wise man said, 'And during this next hour, I would like you to notice the fine artwork. But take care of the oil and do not spill a single drop.'

"This time the young man was in awe of the fine art that he saw. There were giant tapestries from the finest artisans in the world. As his hour was nearly up, he looked down at the spoon. All the oil was gone! He had spilled the precious oil as he preoccupied himself with the castle's splendor.

"With great humility and embarrassment, he returned to the wise man. 'What did you think of my collection?' the wise man asked. 'It is magnificent!' replied the young man. 'But what has become of the oil I entrusted to you?' The young man hung his head in shame. 'I am sorry, but while admiring your fine tapestries, I was not mindful and I spilled the oil.' 'So now I will answer your question,' the wise man said, 'The secret to happiness and success in life is to enjoy all that the world has to offer, to enjoy your journey, but all the while, to be mindful not to spill the oil of life. That is the secret.'"

A SIMPLE CHOICE

"Thank you, Arty, that is exactly what I needed to hear. I will be mindful of maintaining a sense of balance in my life this time around. I understand the message. I will see you next week for lunch." *He knew I knew. Life is about balance.*

I reached for my journal:

April 25, 1999 – Office – 6:30 PM
Promote from within. Begin with Ron. Send the message that as we grow and as job opportunities open up, he should offer them internally to the right guys. As hard as it might be to lose a top technician from his current job, it will be worse to lose him permanently from the company. Perhaps having the technicians we promote teach others might be a way to keep them, too? Ron as a sales rep for maintenance? Who would train him? I have some time, but not the kind he needs...

Page 552. Let's see, what do I remember? "If you have a resentment toward someone, pray for that person for two weeks. Even if you don't mean it, do it anyway for 14 days. You will find that simple discipline will change the way you see the world."

The secret to life? Is it BALANCE? Enjoy the beautiful artwork, but at the same time, don't spill the oil. Perhaps I should donate a portion of my profits and time to the halfway house idea.

Keep writing in my journal. I need to borrow boldly from the best.

Capture ideas and think about how to improve them.

R2A2 = Recognize the principle; relate it to my business.

Assimilate into our systems; apply just one idea.

Empower my employees to integrate that one idea into our daily disciplines.

Reward the behavior I want repeated. Acknowledge and incent sales behavior with my associates.

Chapter 14

Ultimate Goal Achievement

As we sat sipping a latte in Starbuck's, I watched Franklin's face as he listened to my chatter. I must have sounded like a five-year-old, rattling off thoughts and ideas and questions. I didn't care. He was listening intently and it felt good. I told him about my conversation with Arty, about promoting from within, about my experiment with praise and Ron's excitement. I told him that "balance" was the new watchword in our company. He smiled at me in the same way my father had smiled at me while I was growing up. The smile said, "I am so glad you are discovering these great truths on your own; I am proud of you." My father would hold that particular smile for special occasions, such as when I had successfully applied some aspect of his teaching to basketball. For Franklin, I could tell, it was his "psychic pay," that helper's high. He was clearly enjoying the process.

"Tell me what you know about the power of goals," Franklin said.

"Well, I used to set them for sports. When I first started this business, I attended a seminar where the speaker talked about the power of setting goals. I wrote my goals on a yellow legal pad and kept them in my desk drawer. I was always a little embarrassed to show these to anyone. I was amazed that I wrote down five goals for the year while I was at that seminar, and by Thanksgiving of that same year, I had accomplished four of those goals! I was hooked on how well this worked back then, but it's been a while since I've taken the time to set goals. You know, I'm up to my neck in alligators and there's little or no time to drain the swamp."

"When was the last time you carved out some solitude time and wrote down your objectives for the year or even for the next five years, Mister Mike?" Franklin asked softly.

"It's been years, Franklin. I can't remember exactly when I last did it. Perhaps the year after that first year. Maybe six years ago?"

"Would you like to hear a *different* reason to capture a compelling goal on paper?" Franklin asked.

"I would," I said, pen in hand.

"*For what it will make of you to achieve the goal,*" he whispered. Whenever Franklin wanted to make a point, he lowered his voice and leaned toward me. It was like two women whispering in the kitchen about a secret family recipe.

"The greatest reason for setting exciting goals is for what you will learn, and for the person you will have to become in order to achieve those goals."

"I don't understand, Franklin," I said.

"What was the make and model of your first car, Mister Mike?" Franklin asked.

"A nineteen seventy-three Datsun twelve hundred, used," I said, a bit embarrassed. He smiled.

"Then what did you move up to?" he asked.

"A nineteen sixty-nine Volkswagen van, 'The Magic Bus,'" I said, somewhat proudly.

"Wasn't it extraordinary how many VW vans you noticed the first month or two you had that new machine? They were everywhere." His excitement grew with each sentence.

"Yes!" I said, "They were all over the place, it was amazing. I had never noticed them while I had the Datsun."

A SIMPLE CHOICE

"Exactly!" Franklin said. He could tell I was learning.

"Each of us has a series of web-shaped cells at the back of our brains called the reticular activating system. Its sole function is to find profitable data. Your RAS lets in information that helps you along the way toward following your interests." Franklin was having as much fun teaching as I was having learning.

"Once you set a goal and *commit* to it with all your heart and soul, the conversations, ideas, hunches, books, articles, people, systems, methods, and energy just come flying toward you at an astonishing pace."

I knew exactly what he meant. "Go on," I said, not wanting to miss a moment.

"Once we set a compelling goal and begin to move toward that goal, it simultaneously begins to move toward us. The only thing we need know for certain is WHAT we want and WHY we want it. The HOW is not important."

"I know exactly what you mean!" I said. "May I tell *you* a story, Franklin?"

"By all means, Mister Mike," he said.

"When I was in junior high, I had set a goal to improve my grades. Basketball was in my future and I had a strong motivation for raising my grades; playing time!

"I decided I was going to raise my grade in English from a D to an A! It was a single-minded goal. One of my ideas was to get a typewriter. This was before personal computers were affordable. I wanted an IBM Selectric with automatic erase. My mom squashed my idea by telling me that a good used one cost five hundred dollars! I was devastated at first; I had just fifty-eight dollars in savings, but I wouldn't give up. I wanted that typewriter for my school reports and my homework. A month went by with no luck. Then fortune smiled my way. I had volunteered to clean up at our church one Saturday. Rick was the youth pastor and he was coordinating the project. We walked down a hallway filled with a pile of debris. There were flagpoles, old desks, file cabinets from nineteen-forty or so. And there, alone in a corner, sat an IBM Selectric! I asked Rick if I could have it. He said, 'It's all junk. You haul it away and it's yours. It's missing parts, though. Good luck.' I took that old machine to a local business where they sold and fixed used office equipment. The clerk said that it just needed a new ball, a ribbon, and a good cleaning. 'How much,' I asked. Fifty-eight dollars, with the tax! All my homework was typed from that day on."

"That's such a wonderful story," Franklin said. "What I heard you say was you don't need to know HOW, only WHAT and WHY, right, Mister Mike?"

"Right!"

"Suppose you could, on a regular basis, find fifty-eight-dollar typewriters," Franklin said. Then, once you're convinced that the process is sound, you teach your people to find their own fifty-eight-dollar typewriters, and for their own reasons."

"That would be fantastic. You believe it's possible, to show others in my company to do that? I mean metaphorically," I said.

"Of course. Suppose you conduct 'Lunch and Learns' once a month, with a new topic each month? When you invest in education, you always get a return. The return on investment is in direct proportion to the leader's involvement and belief in the time and money. According to Motorola, there's a thirty-to-one return on investment with employee education. The best companies see business education as an investment."

"You mean hiring consultants?" I asked.

"Not if you are uncomfortable with that idea. You can begin by doing it yourself. What about your top technicians?"

"Like Ron," I said.

"Exactly!" he said. "Start 'Johnson University'. Suppliers and some manufacturers are more than ready and willing to assist you. In fact, the more-enlightened distributors will allow you the use of their facilities and equipment for training. You only need ask. The manufacturers want the wholesalers to sell more boxes and parts. They will help you grow your business. If I were you, I would take them to lunch and ask. Just ask."

I was reeling from this conversation. It was so simple, so straightforward. Johnson University! What a great idea! What a great strategy to attract new employees and keep the good ones I have.

"I just know most of my smaller competitors are not doing what we are talking about." I said.

"I would hazard a guess that some of your larger ones aren't either," Franklin said. Mister Mike, just pick up the baton and run with it!

"What if we invited customers, key customers," I said.

"Like Steve Blackburn?" Franklin interjected.

"Exactly!" I knew I would not be able to sleep that night.

The meeting with Franklin lasted until almost 9:30 that evening.

"Eventually you will want to outsource education and bring in specialists. You know, authors, speakers, and consultants. Time will be a big issue. Delegating occasionally will ease your burden. Remember, we get what we pay for. Those authors regularly speak at trade shows and association gatherings. Pay attention and ask around. They will show up in your life."

My head was spinning from all the ideas. I finally drifted off at 3:30 in the morning.

I didn't hear my alarm and overslept. By this time, I had developed a morning ritual. Here are the seven daily disciplines I engage in every day before breakfast:

- Prayer, spiritual text, and reflection (10-15 minutes)
- Review my goals aloud three times a day (10-15 minutes)
- Planning 48 to 72 hours ahead (30 minutes)
- Study and read books that are in alignment with my goals (30-60 minutes)
- THINKING on paper in my journal (15-30 minutes)

- Work out (swim or walk on alternate days)
- Work smart and in a focused way for six to ten hours

I did it faithfully each day. In my reading, I came across these quotes on goals and entered them in my journal:

May 2, 1999

We become what we think about. If it's worth achieving, it's worth writing down. Fifty-eight-dollar typewriters are everywhere!

- **A person with a clear purpose will make progress on even the roughest road. A person with no purpose will make no progress even on the smoothest road.**

- **Reasons are the motivating forces that drive us.**

- **5 Great Goals for This Year:**

1. **Set up Johnson University curriculum by contacting suppliers and work out a co-op plan. Start building the first two classes and present them myself:**
   a) Technician sales and lead generation
   b) Maintenance Sales 101
   c) Goal Achievement 101

2. **Pay the employees to attend each session, even if it means paying overtime!**

3. **Reward learning behavior by handing out coupons, offering time off, gift certificates, and plaques for perfect attendance.**

4. **Sit in the front row of each class to send a message.**

5. **Read a book about presentations and public speaking,** *How to Teach Technicians Without Putting Them to Sleep* **by Dan Holohan.**

I arrived at the office at 10:30 A.M. This time, it was for a very different reason than a hangover. I had a *positive* hangover, HOPE! There is a big difference between coming to and waking up. I knew I would probably be up late again, working into the night. The great difference now was that work had become play. My day was no longer interrupted by an afternoon of drinking and blacking out.

I was attending two to three meetings each week, where we read the various AA books, studied, discussed, and dissected. I was growing spiritually, as well. For the first time since the accident, I actually felt like going to church.

Chapter 15

It's Not What Happens...

Franklin began our meeting by asking me, "Did you ever read about James "Cash" Penney? Before I could answer, he launched into another tremendous business story:

"James 'Cash' Penney was still putting in a full day's work when he was well into his nineties, often refusing to even take time out for lunch. He was one of the first business people to call his employees 'associates.' He was known for having said, 'Unquestionably, the emphasis we have laid on human relationships, toward the public service on one hand, and in giving utmost value toward our associates on the other hand.'

"J.C. Penney opened his first dry-goods store in Kemmerer, Wyoming, in nineteen-o-two. He named it 'The Golden Rule'. Why? Here's what Mister Penney said, 'Because the Golden Rule principles are just as necessary for operating a business profitably as are trucks, typewriters, or twine.' By nineteen-o-seven, he owned twenty-two stores, by nineteen fourteen, forty-eight stores, and by nineteen sixteen, there were one hundred twenty-seven J.C. Penney stores!

"In April, nineteen seventeen, Mister Penney published the first issue of 'The Dynamo'; a company newsletter that he hoped would be 'a working kit of ideas and suggestions.' Finding he could not express himself clearly in print, he hired

A SIMPLE CHOICE

Doctor Thomas Tapper to tutor him. Over a year and a half, Doctor Tapper introduced his new pupil to the world of great books, and taught him a vigorous writing style. Eventually, Mister Penney, Doctor Tapper, and Reverend Francis Short, a pastor in Salt Lake City, guided an education department for the Penney Organization, designed 'simply and solely to help'.

"By nineteen twenty-nine, through a commitment to education, growth, and dedication to his Golden Rule philosophy, J.C. Penney locations grew to an astonishing one thousand three hundred ninety-five stores, and that year's profits were over twelve million dollars! He wore a button in his lapel with the letters HCSC on it. Those letters represented 'Penney's Principles.' They stood for: H for Honor, C for Confidence, S for Service, and C for Cooperation.

"Those words came from Penney's 'Original Body of Doctrine.' This contained the company's vision, values, goals and behavior, or what today we call a mission statement. It read,

'One: To serve the public, as nearly as we can, to its complete satisfaction.

'Two: To offer the best possible dollar's worth of quality and value.

'Three: To strive constantly for a high level of service and quality.'

"James Cash Penney had become a very busy 'Servant Leader.' There were speeches to make, real estate to invest in, and he invested heavily in South Florida. As busy as he was, he was not too busy to take time out to read the stock market report on October twenty-three, nineteen twenty-nine. He read it slowly and carefully, for that was the day the company's common stock was listed on the New York Stock Exchange for the first time. The stock closed at one-hundred twenty dollars a share! Six days later, the market crashed and the company stock plummeted to just thirteen dollars a share.

"As the depression deepened, Mister Penney poured over one-and-a-half million dollars into the City National Bank. The bank failed. Finally, to meet his debts, J.C. had to sell his shares in the company. About that time, my father's older brother, who had ascended to be the senior vice-president at J.C. Penney, lost all his savings. He went deeply in debt, and finally committed suicide by jumping out the window of a twenty-five-story office building in New York City."

I was shocked by this connection in Franklin's story, and I looked up from my notes, but he went on.

"Being poor didn't bother J.C. Penney, but the accusations that he had benefited financially from the bank's failure sure did bother him. He was close to a physical-and-mental break-down, so he entered a sanatorium.

"While there, he experienced a spiritual awakening that enabled him to find himself and to go back to work with the organization he had founded. For the first time, James Cash Penney drew a salary.

"Within three years, he was off the payroll and well on his way to rebuilding his fortune. Meanwhile, he was writing books, articles and pamphlets, lecturing to young people, and serving dozens of organizations, whose aims were to benefit mankind. Mister Penney remained Chairman of the Board until nineteen fifty-nine when he stepped down, although still remaining a director."

"That's an amazing story, Franklin."

There was a glow about him after he shared that story. His eyes sparkled.

"Do you know the root word for education, Mister Mike?" I shook my head. "It's *educo*. Do you know what that means?"

"No," I said.

"To pull out or draw from," he said.

A SIMPLE CHOICE

"Do you want to know what I pulled out of your story, Franklin?"

"Yes, please," he said, leaning forward.

"Develop meaningful relationships both internally and externally. Education is an investment and must come from leadership. It's not what happens to me, it is how I respond. Things always look better in time."

"You're a good student, Mister Mike. I am proud of your progress," Franklin said in a gentle whisper.

"Do you mind if I ask you a question, Franklin? It's very personal."

"By all means, go right ahead. At my age, frankness and honesty are prized virtues because, among other things, they save so much time." He paused, smiled and said, "Please..."

"That is the second story you have told me about relatives you have lost, one to alcoholism and the other to business failure...and suicide."

"You want to know how I responded, how I took the loss and profited from it? Is that it?"

"Precisely!" I said. I think he was reading my mind.

"Every experience tells us whether or not we are open to learning. Tragedy, setback, failure, loss, those are the finest teachers we have. Most of us are so lost in grief, in self-pity, and sadness, that we don't seek the larger lesson, the grander view. I have merely gathered up the lessons loved ones have taught me and used them to help others...and to help myself."

"What about the grief? You mentioned self-pity. How do you get over it?"

"I can only speak from my own experience. I let it happen. I experience it fully. It seems to me that what most men have not learned to do, but that women have done since we lived in caves, is to communicate and process their feelings with others. I have always reached out to talk, to journal, and to honor those that I have lost."

"John Donne's poem, the one you wrote in my journal. *'It*

tolls for thee.' What did he mean by that?" I asked.

"What do *you* think he meant?" Franklin lobbed back at me.

"That we only have so much time. We must grieve for the lost ones, but we must also understand that our time on earth is short?"

"Yes," he whispered. "This is the cycle of grief or phases of loss. We must go through them, from first to last. Each must have its time, sometimes more than once. Time takes time. Those cycles are: shock, anger, bargaining, sadness, acceptance, and *forgiveness.*"

I was silent for what seemed like an hour.

"That makes a lot of sense, Franklin. I found myself going back and forth between anger and sadness. It's been more than a year since I lost my family and I am finally in acceptance. I must admit, though, I don't know if I can ever get to forgiveness."

"Then you will never find peace, Mister Mike, the true peace that comes of forgiveness."

I thought of Arty, and how he prayed for his ex-partner. Maybe I can do this. I don't know.

I had much to think about that night. My journal had become, next to Franklin, my closest friend, my trusted companion.

June 6, 1999

On FORGIVNESS

I must learn how to pray for the guy who took away my family. Maybe I can pray for the willingness to pray for him...I'll give that a try.

A SIMPLE CHOICE

J.C. Penney:

What an amazing story and with so many lessons:

1. **Education from the top down, accomplished with help.**

2. **Written vision, values, goals, and behavior, a code of conduct, defined and modeled.**

3. **Create an acronym for those values and wear it proudly, promote and teach it regularly.**

4. **Learn to deal with setbacks and disappointment.**

5. **Do what you love and love what you do.**

6. **Treat other ASSOCIATES with dignity and respect.**

7. **Relationships—both internal and external—will make or break my company.**

Chapter 16

The Highest Good

The next morning over coffee at Starbuck's, Franklin asked, "Did I ever tell you the story of my old friend, Terence Smith?"

"No," I smiled, getting ready to take notes. I figured he was only going to tell it once, and as it turns out, I was right.

"Terence lived in Bangor, Maine. When I first met him, I must admit, I didn't care for him much. He was arrogant, caustic, cynical, and abrasive. Other than that, he was a pretty good guy." Franklin winked and gave me a slow smile, like the sun breaking through cumulus clouds.

"The first thing I noticed when I visited his office were three plaques with quotes. The first one read, 'I don't meet the competition, I crush it!', the motto of Charles Revson. The second one read, 'You have undertaken to cheat me. I will not sue you, for the law takes too long. I will ruin you!' and was attributed to Cornelius Vanderbilt. The third was Joseph Kennedy's oft-quoted, 'Don't get mad, get even.'"

"A pretty intense guy," I said.

"To say the least. Winning was the name of the game for this man. He once told me 'win' came from the Anglo-Saxon word *winnan,* which means to strive, labor, fight, or struggle. To him, winning wasn't enough, though, someone else had to lose. He was one of those guys who would rather be right than be happy. There was not much joy in his life. Oh, he had amassed a great deal of money, but not an ounce of happiness. He had a large bank account but he also had bleeding ulcers, headaches, and the lot. You see, Mister Mike, there is always someone willing to stay up a little longer, work a little harder, do it a little cheaper. It's difficult to overstate the pervasive influence of win/lose thinking in our lives. As children, we learn at an early age in school, and through sports, that winners are rewarded, and losers are made to feel that, by not winning, they have failed. The message, and it's loud and clear, is, *'The whole world loves a winner.'*"

"What else is there besides win/lose?" I asked.

"A great question, Mister Mike. Here it is, and you can take your choice. It's a simple choice. You have win-lose, lose-win, lose-lose, and *win-win*."

"Win-win? As in mutual profitability? I like that one."

"Yes, mutual profitability, exactly." Franklin was just getting warmed up. "Do you remember the '70s television show *Kung Fu*?"

"The one starring David Carradine as an eastern priest traveling in the Wild West?"

"That's the one. Bruce Lee came up with the idea for that show. He intended to star in it when he submitted it to the studios. What he didn't count on was the studios weren't quite ready for a Chinese-American to break into mainstream American television. Kung Fu was based on a combination of Jeet Quan Do, and Zen philosophy. If you recall, Caine, the character played by Carradine, would walk into a conflict in every episode, and ultimately show everyone 'a better way,' a third alternative to win-lose or lose-win. He would say, 'There is an alternative. There is a third way and it's not a combination of the first two ways. It's a different way.'"

"I am ready, Franklin. What is it?" I asked.

"It demands breaking out of ingrained habits of thinking. It is found by asking the question, *'What is the highest good for all concerned?'*"

I wrote down the question. Franklin paused, as he had dozens of times before. He continued once I finished writing.

"If the solution is best for all, then you have found *mutual profitability*. It is really a way of life, based upon creation of harmony. It requires in equal measure: assertiveness, empathy, intuition, flexibility, and deep thought. It is a new way of seeing how relationships of all kinds can be more fulfilling and satisfying. It means becoming 'other-centered.' It's an extension of Servant Leadership.

"Can this new way of thinking be used in my personal *and* professional life?" I asked.

"By all means. Our business—and personal—lives are not as separate as they might seem. In fact, both areas have one key element in common. In business, as in our personal lives, relationships matter more than anything else. With win-win, relationships are the bottom line. If we can create winning relationships for everyone, success will naturally follow in every area of our lives."

"So, it's a unique way of redefining success in our life?" I said.

"Exactly! That's what Terence had to learn the hard way. After nine lawsuits, seven of which he lost, he had a heart attack. While lying in the hospital, I had a chance to talk with him. He told me that he had a dream one night in which his father came to him and asked him why he was travelling the wrong path. He said this dream was so real to him. His father had been a great man, and he lived this win-win philosophy. Terence told me that his father spoke to him at length. When he woke up, he wrote down everything his father had said to him in the dream. It totaled more than one hundred pages in his journal. He spent the rest of his life trying to live that doctrine of mutual profitability."

"So you learned this from him, or rather, from his father?"

A SIMPLE CHOICE

"Yes," Franklin said in the most solemn tone I had ever heard him use. It was as though this was the most important thing he had told me to date. I leaned forward.

"The purpose of business is to find and keep customers and to make a fair profit," he said. "To provide goods or services that people need, to find a need and fill it. These goods and services are merely a delightful excuse to develop relationships and to serve people. Operating income is nothing more than a reflection of how well you are serving people. Your personal income will be in direct proportion to the quality and quantity of services rendered. Seen in this way, business takes on a different perspective, doesn't it?"

"Yes, it's almost spiritual in nature." I said.

"Yes, it is. Does that make you uncomfortable, Mister Mike?"

"No, not at all; it's just a very different way of looking at the game of business, and life itself."

"Indeed it is," Franklin said. "After he recovered from his temporary setback, Terence began to ask and answer the questions, 'What is in the best interest of our associates?' There must be a better way, what is it?' If good relationships are hidden assets, how can I improve them with my associates, my suppliers, my customers?' He began to solicit thoughts and ideas from his employees. It took a little time, but within a year, most of the people in his company began thinking and acting in this new way. Some people left the company, but he replaced these with others who thought in this win-win way."

"The laws of attraction?"

"Have I told you that story before?" Franklin asked.

"No, but I see where you are going. Please continue!"

"Hidden assets are maximized from these improved relationships. Terence began to foster goodwill. He began to sow seeds of future success. I like to call it 'thinking of the fourth sale first'."

"By that, you mean the long-term relationship?"

"Yes," Franklin said with a smile. "Increased profits are an effect. Low turnover is an effect. High morale is an effect. Increased market share is an effect. Long-term relationships are the key. Breakthrough relationships are long-term business assets. Terence learned, by trial and error, that life and business do not have to be a zero-sum game."

"When you say a zero-sum game, do you mean like poker," I asked.

"Exactly! One of the keys to this new way of life is that I stop playing the 'Comparison Game', and instead play golf. Do you golf, Mister Mike?"

"I used to. It took up too much time."

"I recently shot my age, eighty-four. The key for me was to play against my own best score for that course, and not against the people I happened to be with at the time. I stopped comparing and competing with others. Instead, I now compete and compare with my own best self. It tends to build my self-respect and esteem. Comparison is really self-judgment. I no longer condemn myself on the golf course of life. 'Am I making measurable progress in reasonable time?' That's the key question."

"You have come up with a different way to score," I said.

"I have!" Franklin said with gusto. He smiled and paused, allowing me time to run with the idea.

"The problem, though," I said, "is that there is no end to competition and zero-sum games. It takes more and more *winnan* over people in order to help you feel good about yourself. A little is never enough. It's sort of like booze, very addictive."

"You're in the flow, Mister Mike. You have caught Terence's wave; keep riding it to shore."

I was visibly excited. I sat up straighter and said, "If I change the rules, and if I begin to compete and compare with my own best self rather than with others, I can have a lot more fun, joy, and fulfillment in my business and in my life."

Franklin looked at me for a long moment and then said,

A SIMPLE CHOICE

"Remember to continuously ask and answer the simple questions, 'What is in the highest good of all concerned?' That's the key question."

June 15, 1999

What is the highest good?

Compete and compare against my own best self, rather than against others.

The purpose of business is to find and keep customers; make a fair profit so I might increase my service to others.

Chapter 17

Attitude is a Daily Choice

I was working as hard on my spiritual—and personal—development as I was working on my business, and it was paying huge dividends. Broken relationships and strained relationships healed almost by magic. I was in awe.

Steve Blackburn was very receptive to allowing us to earn back his business. We were having lunch with Arty when he explained, "I believe in second chances, guys. Whenever I have received them, I've made the most of them. I like you, Mike. I believe you are honest and hardworking. You have some great people working for you, and besides, I want to see Franklin again. I miss him."

"I feel a little guilty about that," I said. "After all, he was working for you when I first met you." My toothy grin was tough to hide.

"Don't feel guilty, Mike," Steve said. "There's enough of Franklin to go around. Before he left, he gave me this quote, framed just as you see it." He handed the framed quote to me across his big cherrywood desk. It read:

A SIMPLE CHOICE

"Attitude

"The longer I live, the more I realize the impact of Attitude on life. Attitude to me is more important than the past, than education, than money, than circumstances, than failures, than successes, than what other people think, say, or do. It's more important than appearance, giftedness, or skill. It will make or break a company, a church, or a home. The remarkable thing is we have a choice every single day regarding the Attitude we will embrace for that day. We cannot change the past, we cannot change the fact that people will act in a certain way. The only thing we can do is play on the string we have and that string is our Attitude. I am convinced that life is ten percent what happens to me and ninety percent how I respond to it. I am in charge of my Attitude."

I smiled. So like Franklin.

"That's amazing," I said. "So eloquent and profound."

"I read it everyday," Steve said. "It keeps me focused. Please thank Franklin for me. He was only with me for a few months, but he left quite an impression. Not a day goes by that someone doesn't mention his name. It's uncanny."

"I know what you mean, Steve," I said. "We are delighted to have him."

Steve came back into the Johnson Air family of customers. We were glad to have him. Over the next six months, we picked up another five buildings that he owned, all similar in size and scope. The business in annual maintenance revenue was well over $200,000. Out of that base of business came another $800,000 in repairs and negotiated projects. One million dollars from one relationship! Amazing!

In truth, this all came indirectly from Franklin. Like a giant apple tree bearing buckets of fruit each year, Franklin was everyone's Johnny Appleseed. I had a feeling this was not the first time he had helped someone like me. I was to find out later that my Appleseed analogy would be truer than I could have imagined.

How could I ever thank this guy? He comes into my life, on at least two occasions, intercedes on my behalf, and literally saves my life. On several other occasions, he shows up with "Just the right parts." What is his story?

He has revealed very little of his personal life, his family, other than two lost relatives, and he's reluctant to talk about them. I am afraid it is a painful story, and I hesitate to ask for fear of dredging up a painful past. At times, I catch a glimpse of sadness in his eyes, and that tells me there is a story.

Sara is one of our newest "associates" in accounts payable. She is usually very shy. I was pleasantly surprised when she dropped a note my desk,

"Saw this and thought of you, Mike. We are all proud of your growth. Enjoy. Sara." I read:

How Do You Know It's Bad?

There is a story of an old man who lived in a small village in China. He was the town wise man. The people in the village would come to him for advice and to hear his unique perspective on life. He had one child, a son he had late in life. The son was now in his early twenties and he had many friends. The old man also had a stable of horses. One day his prize stallion ran off. Two of his son's young friends came by to commiserate. 'It's too bad the stallion ran off. We are sorry. The old man smiled and said, 'How do you know it's bad?' The young men walked away, shaking their heads.

The next day the stallion returned with TWO mares at his side. The young men came by to celebrate the good news. The old man smiled and asked, 'How do you know it's good?' Puzzled, the young men left again.

The next day his only son broke his leg while working with one of the mares. The two young men knew *this* would

be bad news. They came by and said in a sad tone, 'Surely, your only son's accident is bad, yes? The old man smiled and simply asked, 'How do you know it's bad?' The two young men left, realizing that they knew nothing.

The next day a warlord came through the village, conscripting all the able-bodied young men for a dangerous and potentially fatal battle. The old man's son with his broken leg was not able-bodied and could not go. The old man just smiled as the two young men walked by without asking any questions. The moral of this story?

Situations and circumstances are neither good nor bad, but thinking makes them so.

In a little less than a year, I had filled three journals with information. I had the beginnings of what I considered an amazing new philosophy for my life. I knew that many of these ideas were not new, but they were certainly new to me.

My journal had become a depository for quotes, ideas, stories, processes, articles, conversations, and observations. I was forming my own philosophy, largely from my expanded associations and the quality of my learning.

I was indeed borrowing from the best. I was reading at least five trade magazines each month. I also read the business section of at least three daily papers: the *Wall Street Journal*, the *New York Times*, and the *Seattle Times*. I had become a sponge. I could feel the difference and others began to notice.

I was now listening to CDs while driving. I was teaching a class once a week at Johnson University. At least once each month, I was attending seminars from a host of rich resources. I was the guy taking notes in the front row. In one year, I attended a business writing class, a DDC-controls class, a personal-development weekend retreat, a leadership conference, a self-esteem workshop, a public-speaking seminar that lasted three days, a workshop on keeping a journal, and I was heading the education committee for the Building Owners and

Managers Association in Seattle. To top it all off, I enrolled in a four-week cooking class!

I granted virtually every request for education. Even more amazing was that some of my people, as a result of my commitment, were attending seminars on their time and expense. Maya Angelou, the great poet, once said, "We train animals, we educate people." I was getting the education that I had always dreamed of. What excited Franklin was the simple fact that everyone around me was also getting the education they had always dreamed of, as well.

I joined a national organization of independent contractors that was committed to growing both their people, and their business. We fostered dispatcher seminars, sales seminars, financial classes, and customer service excellence.

Who would have predicted that the company would grow rapidly, but wisely, at just over 20 percent a year for the next five years? We went from 20 people doing $1,500,000 in business, and losing $300,000 a year, all the way to $18,000,000 a year in service at twenty-percent net profit, for a mind boggling $3,600,000 in profits!

The best part was everyone in the company shared in the gain. Turnover was at an all-time low—less than five percent a year—and morale was through the roof. People were actually waiting to come to work for us. This was unprecedented in our industry. I never could have imagined that this would all happen back on the day I held my father's gun in my hand.

We had adopted the Scanlon Plan. This is a simple plan by which anyone who comes up with an idea that lowers costs or increases sales, shares in the resulting gain. Sometimes, the reward came in the form of a four-day trip, or simply in cash. Trade magazines, local newspapers, and even a national magazine had written about us. Life was good!

Ron was selling his socks off. He closed more business in six months than I had ever closed in a year. He sold over $400,000 in maintenance sales! I knew that the next promotion for him would be to sales manager. If we could transfer his passion and knowledge to others, I knew that he would be the most happy and fulfilled guy we had. Helping him see his future as clearly as I could see it was the Pygmalion Principle that Franklin had taught me. Ron was my "Eliza" and he was a joy to behold. I realized that releasing human potential is one of the great gifts of leadership.

Whenever I saw Ron, I asked him how it was going. He always answered with one of these wonderful statements: "A notch above awesome, Mike!", "Incredible and getting better every minute!", or "I am on this side of the grass and grateful!"

My favorite, though, was, "Fluctuating between fabulous and sensational; I just keep drifting back and forth!"

This was the guy who never finished high school. He dropped out of Wailea High School in Hawaii at 17 and joined the Marines. I found him during his first year out of the military. He was hungry, eager, and willing to work hard. Ron had grown up in a broken home, with an alcoholic father who beat him with regularity. Once we had gotten to know each other, he slowly shared memories of his childhood, one by one. It was like a dentist pulling teeth, but each time he shared a part of his past, it cut the intensity in half and the healing was now almost complete.

I followed a simple formula: In helping Ron, I was allowing myself to face my own fears and demons. Observing life, and vicariously living his experiences, produced two reactions in me. The first was relief and gratitude for not having experienced some of the things that others have experienced, such as what Ron had gone through, for instance. The second was the recognition that another's life, observed from the outside, has a shape and definition to it that is lacking in one's own life. I felt that way about Franklin.

Franklin taught us all a great deal about mental management, and how to foster and maintain a great attitude. His able example was like a positive contagion that swept through our little company. It was a virus that we were all grateful to catch.

Smiling became a habit, as did positive and sincere praise. Catching others in the act of doing things well was a daily occurrence. Capturing WINS, in the form of letters of gratitude from customers, made their way onto the walls of the company. We called it our "Wall of Fame." Our most high-profile customers' buildings, and the letters they sent us, hung from our walls like a hunter's trophies. Pride in people and performance was the order of the day. We had one entire wall of pictures dedicated to our technicians and their families. We had two parties each year, one on July Fourth and another during the Christmas holiday season. Clowns painted the faces of children during the summer. Franklin, with apron and chef's hat, flipped burgers and hot dogs, the ever present unlit cigar in his mouth. We had three-legged races and egg tosses and the children loved it. So did I. We all did. And we captured it all on film.

We became an employer of choice in our region. I was proud of our people. I was proud of what our company was becoming. And my journal was growing daily. I found myself pasting quotes such as these into it:

July 3, 1999

"Servant Leadership is a paradox. It's counter-intuitive. The leader serves the people he works with as an attendant, a steward, and a model of humility, grace, kindness, and empathy."

"The strongest principle of growth lies in the human choice." —George Eliot

"How do you know it's bad?" —Chinese proverb

"We have a choice every single day regarding our attitude for that day."

Chapter 18

You Don't Need to Be Sick to Get Better

I was so excited to book the business Ron had just closed that we skipped lunch. As we drove to the shop, Ron smiled at me and pulled out his worn copy of Charlie "Tremendous" Jones' classic, *Life is Tremendous*.

Franklin greeted us at the door. "Mister Mike, you look very content, sort of like the cat that ate the canary!"

"Is it that obvious?" I said. "Ron just closed another one hundred thousand dollars' worth of business with Steve Blackburn's company! Let's celebrate!"

Ron never even looked up. He was lost in *Life is Tremendous*. "Good book, Ron?" He didn't even hear Franklin's question. Franklin gently tapped him on the shoulder.

"Oh, Franklin. Sorry. What did you say?"

"Good book?"

"Yes, I found a place that sells great books at wholesale prices. This one's terrific. Here, listen to this:

'You will be the same person in five years, but for two things: the people you associate with, and the books you read.' A cardinal rule to remember in reading inspirational books is that you only get to keep and enjoy what you share and give away. If you aren't going to read with the purpose of sharing and giving, I suggest you give the books to someone who will share, and you will then discover the power of books as you watch the reader grow through sharing with you. Perhaps the best idea would be to use the brain trust idea of *Think and Grow Rich* and both of you begin reading and sharing with each other. "So, I bought all of us copies of these books and had them shipped overnight. What's great is that they're all classics."

"Timeless self-help and business books that never go out of style?" Franklin asked.

"You bet!" Ron said, reaching into a box and handing us each four books: *Life is Tremendous* by Charlie T Jones, *Think and Grow Rich* by Napoleon Hill, *Acres of Diamonds* by Russell Conwell, and *How to Win Friends and Influence People* by Dale Carnegie.

I smiled. Ron was infected with a positive contagion. "So, you think we should start a Book-of-the Month club within the company?"

"Absolutely!" Ron said, "You read my mind!"

We all began reading 30 minutes each morning, and at odd moments throughout the day. Learning had become a corporate way of life.

Listening to audio books became a regular habit for us as well. Most of us had at least a 30-minute commute, and that translated into an hour of daily learning.

We each got through one new audio book, typically six audios per program, every week: Zig Ziglar and Brian Tracy on selling, Roger Dawson on negotiating, Earl Nightingale's *The Strangest Secret*, and Don Shula and Ken Blanchard on coaching. We became sponges. One quote that really stuck with us; it was from Bob Moawad, "You don't need to be sick to get better." It became our catch phrase.

As the coach goes, so goes the team. We had all the coaches on the high road to knowledge. We were rapidly becoming a learning organization.

Chapter 19

Service to Others

Franklin, Ron, Jeremy Travers—a service tech who worked his way up from the bottom to become our service manager—and I became inseparable. We met twice a week to discuss a variety of things, mostly about how to grow the business. We had formed our own "Mastermind Group," as Napoleon Hill of *Think and Grow Rich* fame called it.

We were beginning to think that maintenance sales were the way to grow our business in both good times and bad. Franklin said in one meeting, "The ironic thing is that in times of economic slowdown, the most enlightened business leaders have always understood that you should invest MORE discretionary capital from your budget into the SERVICE-sales side of the business. Sales training in an economic downturn is an investment."

We developed a little motto that ended up framed on each person's desk. We put the same on an laminated index card for each technician:

"When all else fails, think Maintenance Sales!"

Franklin ran his hands through his hair. It was time for a story:

"Elisha Graves Otis was born in eighteen eleven, and worked his way up to a job in a machine shop in Yonkers, New York. In the early eighteen fifties, he set about to increase the safety of steam-driven hoists. Up until then, these relied on ropes and pulleys, which were both liable to break. Mister Otis had a great idea. He attached a spring between the hoist car and the rope. If the rope broke, the spring would activate brake shoes, which lodged in the notches cut into the rails that framed the hoist shaft.

"Otis had an opportunity to demonstrate his new invention at the eighteen fifty-three New York World's Fair. Once an hour, with the assistance of master salesman P.T. Barnum, Mister Otis would step onto the hoist platform. When it rose up the shaft at the rate of twelve feet per minute, he brandished a sword and slashed the rope. It was quite a show. Needless to say, the marketplace responded. Mister Otis sold and installed three elevators for three hundred dollars. An industry was born.

"With the help of his two sons, he installed the first high-rise elevator in eighteen seventy-one. By eighteen eighty-one, Otis Elevators was carrying some fifty million people, and without one incident! In eighteen eighty-seven, they sold five hundred sixty-eight elevators. The company won the contract to install the elevator in the famous Eiffel Tower in France. By eighteen ninety-eight, Mister Otis emerged as a consolidator and bought up rival companies. The company went public, and was poised to take advantage of Edison's new invention, electricity."

Franklin was on a roll. His eyes were shining. He ran his hand through his hair. I smiled. He took a deep breath and continued.

"Otis Elevator was in the right place at the right time. At a time of unprecedented growth and expansion, the company grew with the advent of steel and high-rise buildings. Then, the Great Depression hit. At the time, Otis Elevator employed nineteen thousand five hundred people. Half were laid off and new sales fell to a trickle.

A SIMPLE CHOICE

"To find an alternative, the company made a strategic move that many other large companies have since copied. For nearly eighty years, the company had considered transactions complete with installation of a new elevator. There were, of course, occasional sales of spare parts and inspections of elevators, which contributed to company revenues, but in the depths of the Depression, the company was forced to look hard at its business. As a result, they began to focus more on service and maintenance and less on new sales.

"Between nineteen twenty-nine and nineteen thirty-six, as the economy stagnated, maintenance contracts rose thirty percent. During the nineteen thirties, elevator service brought in more revenue than new sales. By nineteen fifty-five, service accounted for forty-three percent of total sales! In nineteen seventy-five, when revenue reached one billion dollars, United Technologies purchased the company."

"The same company that owns the Carrier Corporation?" Ron asked.

"Yes," Franklin said, "the same. Now, in nineteen ninety-nine, Otis Elevator has revenues of five billion six-hundred million dollars and sixty-six thousand employees, mostly built on service." He smiled, content with the impact of his story.

Franklin had done it again. So many points made in one terrific story of business success, and I understood the main point: SERVICE is the key. It's the straightest way to steady profits. It provided cash in lean times and the ability to offer a no-furlough policy to employees. So simple, and yet so often overlooked.

Ron looked at me for support and then said, "Franklin, with your help, do you think we could come up with a five-year maintenance sales plan for the company's growth?"

"It would be my pleasure, Ron. It's easier than you think. Let's put it on paper. By capturing what you want on paper, a number of things happen. It's the "Law of Focus." Whatever we focus upon increases and always grows larger in our lives.

Whatever we disregard or ignore diminishes. By insinuating these words into your subconscious daily, and then sharing them with the people in your organization, you manifest it into being." Franklin said this with such confidence and authority. I believed him and so did Ron. It was tangible and it was exhilarating.

"We become what we think about," I said.

"Exactly," Franklin said. "Turn everyone into an advocate and become a selling machine. Maintenance sales represent the lifeblood of growth for this future vision. Maintenance sales allow you to plan for manpower scheduling, anticipate hiring needs, teach employees about how our company makes money: top line sales, gross profit, and net profit."

Franklin ran his fingers through his hair. I smiled. It was his little teaching quirk. The thought occurred to me again, *How much time does he have left? I'd better pay attention and savor every moment, every word. I took my father for granted when I was young. I thought he would live forever. I now know differently.*

Franklin interrupted my thoughts, "Though it seems like there are other things that are more important—urgent things, reactive things—be sure to make maintenance sales a daily priority. It will also create the need for a second full-time sales person to deal with negotiated project work that comes from that base of business. For every dollar of maintenance sales, a business can expect an additional three to four dollars in projects and repair sales."

We worked on it for 12 hours and came up with a five-year plan. It was rough, but it was a start. "Eventually," Franklin said, "we'll need to create an organization chart with clearly defined roles and goals."

"Like job descriptions?" I asked.

"Yes," Franklin said. "But let's stay with first things first."

Within 30 days, we made sweeping changes to our profit picture and personnel. Ron had now been promoted to sales manager. He was in early and he stayed late. I was concerned about the time he was spending away from his family, but he assured me that he and his wife, Mary, had talked it through, and agreed that during the first year he would learn as much as he could.

He took a year off from coaching his kids and poured himself into his new position. I admired his commitment and I couldn't argue with his logic; it is what it takes to succeed, to get things going. We had a gentleman's agreement: He would scale back the hours after one year, so as not to neglect family. I never would have done something like that in years past. I was a different man now.

I began to see the changes Franklin had made in me and through me.

Chapter 20

Flying Solo

It was a beautiful Indian summer day in Seattle, unseasonably warm, with temperatures in the low 80s. The nights were crisp and cool. The leaves were turning crimson and gold. There were those persistent groups of leaves that managed to cling to the tree, like a cat hanging by one paw from a branch. It was nature's signal of the shorter days and rainy nights to come. Soon it would be October, but for Franklin, it was already winter.

"I have put my things in order," he said. "The grandson of an old friend helped me draw this up." He slid a manila folder across the table. I shuddered, as if a cold breeze had just blown down my neck.

"Please do not open it until this weekend, Mister Mike. You must promise. It is very important to me that you honor my wish. The chill returned. "What is it, Franklin, your notice? Are you retiring?"

"Not exactly, Mister Mike. If you have the time, I have a story to tell you."

"Franklin, you have all the time you need," I said, but somehow knowing that this wasn't the case, I immediately wished I could take back those words.

He continued in a very serious tone, one I had never before

heard from him. "The year was nineteen thirty-one. I was sixteen years old. I had just graduated from high school and had fallen in love with Isabel Jones. She was smart, focused, driven, self-assured, and tall, with the kind of blond hair that shines in the sunlight, and these piercing blue eyes. As class president, she was certainly the most well-known girl in school. What made her even more intimidating was the fact she was two years older than I was.

"It didn't matter, though. I was in love. It took me almost a year to convince her to go out with me, but by her senior year we were THE COUPLE on campus. The plan was to marry after college graduation. I was a young man in a hurry. I graduated with honors at nineteen, from tiny Eureka College in Illinois."

"Ronald Reagan's alma mater?" I asked softly.

"Yes, Dutch. We played football together. I wasn't very good. You know, too skinny, but my, was I persistent and I worked hard."

"I left Eureka to attend Chicago University where I earned my master's degree in English. By twenty-four, I had my Ph.D., and I accepted a teaching position at the University at Bangor, Maine. By then, Izzy and I had three girls: Sara, who was seven, Ruth, who was five, and little Margaret, who was just three years old. We didn't have much money but we were the happiest family in the world."

There was such sadness in his voice. I dreaded hearing what was to come.

"That winter was particularly harsh. It was nineteen forty-one, December fifth, nineteen forty-one, two days before the Japanese bombed Pearl Harbor. Izzy was driving our old 'thirty-five Ford home from a Christmas-shopping trip to Boston. She never saw this man, Fuller. He ran the stop sign. He had been drinking. They found three pints of bourbon in the back seat of his car. He broadsided their car, smashing it over an embankment. It rolled down the hill, hit a large rock, and folded like an accordion. My entire family was gone, my beloved Izzy, little Sara, Ruth, and baby Margaret. Gone.

"Something died in me that night, Mister Mike. There was no hope. I turned to alcohol for solace. It helped at first. What became clear to me, though, was that if I wasn't mindful, I would follow the same path my brother took. But I didn't care." He stopped to wipe the tears that ran down his face.

"For ten years, I was lost in an alcoholic stranglehold of despair, self-pity, resentment and fear. I was angry toward God. I was angry toward Fuller, the fellow who selfishly took my family from me. I was angry toward myself for not driving them to Boston. I didn't drive them because I was too busy writing my second novel. I had a deadline with my publisher. What I failed to see was that my family was slipping away from me. In my wife's diary after her death, I read all these passages of sorrow and regret."

As Franklin told his story—the one story I had longed to hear—I realized that he had told this intensely personal and private story to only a few people during his long life. I felt privileged and I redoubled my active-listening efforts. This was important for both of us.

"It was December fifth, nineteen fifty-one. I was in jail for being drunk and disorderly in public in a small town near Akron, Ohio. During the night, the sheriff brought in another inmate for the same offense. It took me a while to recognize him. He had been on an identical journey, the proverbial highway to hell, parallel paths. It was Fuller. He had more gray hair and less of it, but it was him, unmistakably. It was him."

I couldn't help but be amazed—astounded—by the similarities between Franklin's experience and my own experiences. Our paths, our journeys, our trials, our afflictions, are so similar, and completely related. No wonder he knew me so well. He had truly been there and done that! He was telling my story from a different time and a different place, but it was my story exactly.

A SIMPLE CHOICE

"This was the fellow who had taken my family from me," Franklin said. "All manner of evil thoughts raced through my head. He was to blame. This was my chance for revenge. He was drunk and asleep. The sheriff was in the other room. I could take his life, and…what was I thinking? I could *never* do that." He raised his head and seemed to be looking at me in his half-conscious drunken stupor. This hung-over man was a lost soul; there was a real sadness about him.

"And it was at that moment that something came over me. Perhaps it was the years of grief and lost time, the anguish of unfulfilled dreams left dying on the snow that fateful night. Like lancing a boil, I let out a bloodcurdling scream. It was so violent that I didn't even recognize it as coming from me. It shook Fuller from his stupor. The sheriff came running in the room. I was sitting on my bunk, head in my hands, weeping. Fuller was rubbing his eyes, as if to say, 'Who woke me up so early?' The sheriff told me to pipe down and left the room, shaking his head. Fuller asked what all the commotion was about. What was it all about? *What was it all about!* I told him to sit still and listen. I talked for more than an hour, and when I was through, I saw a broken man, a man worse off than I was."

"You see," Franklin continued, "Fuller had lost everything. The insurance company sued him personally, and his business as well, and they won. He lost his company and he started drinking daily."

Franklin told me the whole story in painful detail. I listened intently. When he was finished, he wept. I held him.

Franklin sipped some water and then said, "For ten years, he had been in a prison of his own making, far worse than what the state could have ever provided. He suffered more than I had and on every conceivable level. I felt only compassion for him. He had suffered mightily for ten years. Guilt, shame, fear, and remorse had been his constant companions. He had no friends; his wife had divorced him; everyone close to him had deserted him. We finally slept, and that night in jail, I had a dream, an epiphany. It was a dream so real that I awoke in a sweat, as though someone had poured a gallon of water over me. In all my eighty-four years, I have never had another quite like it. To this day, I can recall the entire dream. In it, my Isabel, as an angel of hope, comes to me and tells me that if I want to be free of my anger, resentment, and fear, the answer is to become a business partner to Fuller. I was to help him rebuild his business, but first, I was to help him get and stay sober, no matter what."

I sat in silence, leaning forward, listening.

"I cannot describe the feeling I had, Mister Mike. It was one of absolute *freedom from fear*. It was as though all the pain and anger had been lifted in one great motion. I felt like Ebenezer Scrooge in Dickens' *A Christmas Carol*. I fell to my knees and prayed for forgiveness, first for myself, and then for my new friend, Fuller."

I listened in disbelief. This was too amazing to believe, and yet...

"I invested the next year, working sixteen hours a day, helping him to rebuild his business and his life."

I interrupted for only the second time, "Let me guess, he was a heating contractor?"

"Yes."

I smiled. "Franklin, I am sorry; please continue."

"It is amazing what two people can accomplish if they share the same objectives and purpose. We did the work of ten men, working at breakneck speed during that first year. We established one of the first companies to hire alcoholics and help them become rehabilitated. Akron, Ohio, as you know, was a sort of hub for sobriety in the Forties and Fifties."

"Dr. Bob Smith, one of the co-founders of AA. Wasn't that his hometown?" I asked.

"Exactly!" We had plenty of prospects. AA was still new then, and not particularly well-received by businessmen. There was much skepticism, not like it is today, but we were on a mission. You have never seen such a changed man."

"Fuller?" I asked tentatively. "Your new partner?"

Pausing for a moment, he smiled and said, "Well, yes, him too!"

"Forgiveness is one of life's great secrets," Franklin said. "When the student is ready to learn, the teacher shows up. We taught each other. Mister Mike, one of the things I learned was that you don't have to choke your anger. You only have to surrender your malice. For YOUR sake, malice is misery that needs healing. Anger is energy that needs redirecting. After malice, I let anger do its reforming work. Forgiveness and anger can be partners in a good cause."

Franklin was pulling up memories from the past that were profound in their implications, because these were, I sensed for this one last time, just what the doctor ordered. I had an overwhelming impending sense of closure in this meeting. I clung to his every word.

"Hate turns its power against the hater. It saps the energy of the soul, leaving it weaker than it was before, too weak to create a better life beyond the pain. As a long-term solution, hate is a poor choice. In the end, it kills."

He paused to catch his breath. I leaned forward to catch his words. With each paragraph, his voice grew softer. The candle was going out.

"Forgiveness is the answer, Mister Mike. It's the path to *freedom from fear*. No one can make that choice for you. It's *a simple choice*. Love or hate. Only a free person can choose to start over with someone who has hurt them. Only a free person can live with an uneven score. Only a free person can heal the memory of hurt or hate. Only a free person…"

He was struggling. Each word came a little harder than the last. He was in the last few seconds of his game. We both knew it.

"Could you please get me a glass of water, Mister Mike? I

would be much obliged."

"Of course." I got up to fetch a glass and began to sob, as though turning on the faucet in the sink released all the water of grief, hatred, anger, resentment, self-pity, and fear in me. I wiped away the tears before I went back to hear the rest of the story.

"Fuller and I parted ways after the year was up. That's just how long it took me to heal the wounds and finish the job we started together. In the end, during the last few weeks, I had empowered everyone around me to the point where the only truly useful thing I felt I was doing was driving parts to people on job sites. Oh, sure, I listened. I told a few stories. I listened some more. Mostly I delivered parts."

"Redemption and hope found," I said, with a new tear in my eye. "You found your life's purpose in a simple act of humble service, Franklin Robinson, as a parts driver?" He smiled. "We both know you are much more than that to me and the people at Johnson Air."

"Thank you, Mister Mike. But in the end, all I have ever really been is a parts driver."

"What happened after you left Fuller?"

"Oh, he wanted to give me a great deal of money, partnership, and all that. I couldn't do it. It would have diluted the joy and fulfillment of service. He was very insistent. We finally negotiated a deal. I received a nineteen fifty-two Ford pickup truck and a modest trailer to pull the essentials; you know, books, journals, food, some coveralls, and a straw hat and a built-in humidor."

"What then, you became a gypsy?"

"When I was a boy, I was enamored of the fable of Johnny Appleseed. I would like to believe I planted some pretty good fruit trees in my travels."

Pausing, I leaned forward and whispered, "How many in all, Franklin, fruit trees, I mean?"

A SIMPLE CHOICE

"Let's see, you are number twenty-seven…"

"Twenty-seven? Were they all mechanical contractors?"

"That would have been nice. No, probably twenty or so were. There were janitorial companies, electrical contractors, plumbing contractors, even some carpet-cleaning companies. But the focus was always the same, SERVICE."

"Did all of them have alcohol problems? The owners, I mean?"

"Well, that would have simplified things as well, I suppose. No, some had drug addictions, others gambling problems or eating disorders, but the recovery process and initial emphasis remained the same. Physical recovery first, spiritual and emotional growth second, and then intellectual and interpersonal growth last. Then the business. Servant Leadership was the glue that put the puzzle together. Appreciating the people you are blessed to serve, treating people with love, understanding, and respect. I am afraid I am running out of time, Mister Mike. My race is almost over. I am on my final lap."

That night I wrote in my journal:

November 17, 1999

It's a simple choice. Love or hate. Only a free person can…

And on that night Franklin died of natural causes in his sleep.

Chapter 21

Planting Shade Trees of My Own

It was raining the day of the funeral, not a big surprise in Seattle. The pastor was reading a passage from the Bible, Ephesians 6:7: "Serve wholeheartedly as if you were serving the Lord, not men." That was Franklin.

Funerals have a strange effect on me. I go through a sort of values clarification. I am always reminded of the brevity of life when someone passes on to the Sweet Hereafter. Why is it that funerals remind us just how fragile life truly is? Franklin had lived a good long life by anyone's standards. He was three days short of his eighty-fifth birthday, 13 years past the average lifespan of the American male.

How many people had he helped? Twenty-seven? More like 27 times 270! He had touched so many lives in my company in less than a year: employees, customers, and suppliers, but mostly, he touched me. He left giant footprints in the sand, a massive shade tree that he won't get to sit under. He knew. He was Johnny Appleseed. Fruit trees blossomed all across our country, casting long and broad shadows for years to come.

Just as the pastor concluded his remarks, something amazing happened. The clouds parted and the sun peeked from behind the dark rain clouds, like a child playing peek-a-boo. The rays of sunlight spread like fingers, casting light directly onto the open grave. I wasn't the only one to notice. The other 500-plus people in attendance looked up at that magnificent moment. Then God, as if to say, hold on, there is more, produced a rainbow the likes of which I have never seen.

Perfect. Franklin deserved a rainbow, at the very least, a rainbow. I thought of what Abraham Lincoln had said, "Die when I may, I want it said of me, by those who knew me best, that I always plucked a thistle and planted a flower where I thought a flower would grow." That was Franklin, the gardener, the philosopher, the teacher, the social scientist, the coach, the counselor, the mentor, the man, the parts driver.

Franklin had once handed me a poem, which he suggested I memorize:

"Only one life that soon is past. Only what's done with love will last!"

After the service was over, the sun went behind the clouds again, as if to say, okay, now that we have honored my friend, Franklin, it's time to go back to business as usual. The dark cumulus clouds returned, and once again, it began to rain. Rain in Seattle? For the first time in a long time, I noticed the rain. It bothered me.

I walked slowly back to my car, my tears concealed by the rain. I was feeling much like I felt that day in my office with the Colt 45. The difference between then and now was hope and meaning. I knew I would grieve the loss of my friend and mentor for as long as it took. Today I had a new way of life. I had sound principles by which to live my life. Principles that would keep me challenged for as long as I live. A complete change had taken place in my life. Where I used to run from responsibility, I now accepted it with gratitude. I know that I can shoulder it. Instead of wanting to escape, I find myself gladly tackling life with passion and purpose. I now enjoy the respect of my employees, a wealth of friends, and with my AA friends, an unusual quality of fellowship, first through mutual pain and suffering, and now with a newfound faith and hope.

I got into my truck and turned the ignition. A self-help CD was on the passenger's seat. This day, I was not in the mood for self-help. I wanted to grieve my lost friend. I wanted to feel sad and grieve for my teacher. During the following week, I would lament, weep, mourn, sorrow, suffer, bemoan, and bewail the loss. It was understood. This time it was different.

My parts driver's words come back to comfort me, "Time takes time."

I turned on the radio to hear the Doobie Brothers. "Oh black water, keep on rolling, Mississippi moon won't you keep on shining on me…"

The leaf spring…the phone call…the resume…the parts driver. Franklin had changed my life. I would never be the same again. Being experienced in grief, I knew the world would conspire to remind me of him. I turned the dial to the local jazz station. I was lost in the music and I stared at the gray sky above. The raindrops fell on the windshield providing a cover, a painted veil to insulate me from the outside world.

I had forgotten about the package Franklin had given me the week before. The large manila envelope had slid to the floor of the truck, hiding.

I opened it, and found a letter typed on the same parchment paper, a copy of his will, and a key ring with two lonely keys that seemed out of place, yet, like an old married couple, with history and companionship. I read Franklin's will:

My Dear Friend, Mr. Mike,

As you are reading this, it means that I have gone to the Sweet Hereafter. Please understand I am in a much better place. You will have to wait to see, but we will be together again on God's Golden Shore someday. I will be waiting, having already set a place at the table for nine. You will

A SIMPLE CHOICE

join Isabel, Sara, Ruth, Margaret, Karen, Ian, and Derek, and we will all laugh, hug, smile, reminisce, and be together for all time.

In the meantime, I have a few favors to ask:

1. Please drive up to Concrete (the map is attached) and dispose of my things. Time did not allow me to finish that task. You will find the keys in this package as well. I will leave it to your fine discretion as to which things to keep, and which to dispose of.

2. I have included the number of my attorney, John McDevitt. He is the grandson of an old friend. He has my Last Will and Testament. Please contact him.

I have tried, (at least since that fateful night in jail back in 1951), to stay true to my life's purpose, that is: "To seek adventures for the soul and try and make a difference in people's lives." I never set out to change the world, I leave that up to others who are far more qualified than I am. I am interested, after all, in that one percent, that small fraction of the population, who find themselves at the proverbial crossroads, looking to make the worst kind of deal with the wrong kind of guy. Suicide, by gun or by bottle, are different sides of the same coin. One is much more expedient, but both accomplish the same thing: a soul lost, all opportunity vanquished, and all potential, forever lost.

In some small way, I have tried to invest my time where I thought it would make the most difference. Wherever a man turns, he can find someone who needs him. Watch for the little things to be done, the small parts to be delivered. It requires courage and resilience, Mister Mike, especially in the great cities, do the doors of the heart need to be opened. What stupendous opportunities for service await those who are simply willing to be servants. Often, these kind gestures of the heart are as a single ray of sunshine, piercing a darkness we may not dream is there.

In gratitude for our good fortune, we must render, in return, some sacrifice of our life for another's life. For those of us who have suffered in unique ways, there exist unique opportunities. We can all be rich in love and generosity.

Tenderness and compassion to those who are weaker than us strengthens the heart toward life itself. We do terrible things to each other in the name of justice. The moment we understand and empathize for the other person, we wash ourselves, and the world is cleaner.

Forgiveness! You might ask, why forgive? If I do not forgive, I remain untrue to myself. If I remain untrue to myself, I shall then be acting as if I were innocent of the same offenses. I am not. I must forgive the lies directed at me, because so many times my own conduct has been blotted by lies. I must forgive the heartless, the hatred, the judging, the slander, the fraud, and the arrogant, without noise or fuss. He that attempts to live these principles will know the real adventures and ultimate triumphs of the soul.

I must seek to be the best parts-delivery person I can be. Such a career demands patience, tolerance, devotion, daring, and faith. It calls for strength of will and determination to love; the greatest test of man. It is the only way to true happiness and everlasting joy.

I now pass the baton to you, my friend. You are under no obligation to follow; it is simply an idea. Do you want to make a difference in people's lives? Once you grab hold of this idea, it will become as electricity, you will not be able to let go. So take your time. Ask God for guidance on the idea for a week, and then decide.

It's the most unique path you will ever trod, the most rewarding one I know. Keep working on increasing your service to others. I know you will. Keep raising the bar on yourself and with your associates. This keeps us all green and growing.

In the end, it comes down to a simple choice, Love or Hate, Live or Die. We must give away the hardest-earned lessons in order to keep them. Live each day as though it were your last, for one day, it will be. Work as if you will live forever. Live as if you will die tomorrow.

May God keep you until we meet again, Mister Mike. Remember, for whom the bell tolls...

Your Humble Servant,
Franklin Robinson

P.S.
By some divine fate, God reached down through the sands of time and connected us in a unique way. You see, "Fuller" was Ray Fuller Johnson or R.F. as you knew him, your paternal grandfather. The circle is now complete. You now know the whole story.

Franklin's RV was an Airstream, a truly beautiful piece of American craftsmanship. In fact, it was, without a doubt, the largest, most plush recreational vehicle I had ever seen. Amazing. He drove this old '52 Ford pickup truck, but this thing was quite another story. As I walked in, I estimated its retail value at well over $600,000.

This extraordinary combination of house and automobile was out of character for Franklin. It was neither humble nor subdued. It was downright extravagant!

It had it all: air conditioning, a state-of-the-art stereo with Bose speakers, 15 in all, each strategically placed for optimum effectiveness. The stereo alone was worth well over $10,000 dollars! I smiled at the tapes: Lionel Hampton, Duke Ellington, Sara Vaughn, Louis Armstrong, Chet Baker, Tommy Dorsey,

Benny Goodman, Frank Sinatra, Sammy Davis, Jr., Dean Martin, and Tony Bennett.

There was a knock at the door. A slightly heavyset woman in her mid-50s, wearing a Harley-Davidson tee shirt, black leather jacket, and bleached-blonde hair that bore a striking resemblance to Marilyn Monroe's in every way, stood before me. She was holding a golden lab puppy, and she was smiling.

"He was a very nice man," she said. "The sweetest man in the world. We will miss him. Everyone here loved him." She paused for a moment to size me up, the way a car salesman might, to determine whether you are a good prospect, worthy of his time. "He left this for you," she said, handing me the puppy. "His name is Aristotle. Funny name for a dog, don't you think?" She left without another word.

Aristotle, a funny name? No, that's the perfect name. Just like Franklin. Aristotle was yet another great Greek teacher. He was Alexander the Great's personal mentor for many years, and the founder of the concept of the university. It was perfect.

I didn't have much time to ponder, though. Aristotle turned his head and gave me a big lick on the face. And then he peed on my shirt. Life. Perfect!

Johnson Air has made it onto "One of the 100 Best Small Companies to Work for in America" lists. Of that, I am extremely proud. We have been blessed with great and dedicated people, caring people. We never wanted to be the biggest, only the employer of choice in our state. I believe we are well on our way to achieving our objective. We put a unique twist on leadership. All our associates voted in the next generation of leaders.

We call our annual Independence Day party, "The Franklin Robinson Memorial Barbecue." Everyone comes dressed in coveralls, a straw hat, and bubble gum cigars. Aristotle presides over the affair with dignity and grace, keeping the other dogs in line.

We celebrate birthdays with a cake, a giant card, which

everyone signs, and I lead a rousing version of "Happy Birthday!" If we have guys who are on large projects and cannot come into the shop for cake, we take the party to the jobsite…and embarrass the associate on site!

Our Associate of the Month receives the award with a $500 savings bond for extraordinary customer service above and beyond the call of duty. One technician drove a pregnant facility manager from her office to the hospital, and stayed at the hospital until the baby arrived. They decided to name the baby, Vincent, after our tech!

We offer on-site Doggy and Kiddy Day care. If the dog messes on the carpet three times, he must attend obedience school (the cost of which the company covers) for six weeks. Aristotle was the first successful graduate of that esteemed academy. You can teach a new dog new tricks. Old dogs, too.

We offer bonuses for recruiting new employees, $1,000 in cash or savings bonds, or a time-off equivalent. Most seem to take the time-off option. Management covers for the associates fifty percent of the time. Eighty percent of the best ideas come from our associates.

Time does not allow us to list all we do, but Franklin's spirit lives on in the halls of Johnson Air. There is a beautiful oil painting of him in the lobby, right next to our Vision Statement, "Making a Difference in People's Lives though Extraordinary Service!"

John McDevitt had an impressive resume and a law degree from Harvard. He was originally from Maine and he looked a lot like young Robert Redford.

He smiled broadly as he unraveled the leather cord that held the leather attaché together. It was something right out of late Victorian England. He removed a piece of the same parchment paper I had seen many times before, Franklin's signature paper of choice.

"Mr. Johnson, this will be a brief meeting. There are only two items in the will." He leaned forward and handed me a cashier's check for $10 million dollars. I sat frozen, stunned. I kept looking at the zeroes, seven in total. I had never held or seen that many goose eggs on one piece of paper.

"What does this mean? Why . . . " I couldn't finish my sentence.

John paused, smiling as he leaned forward, "Simple. Franklin never accepted money from any of the people he helped over the years. To thank him, most of the people he helped bought either savings bonds or stock in his name, and almost all of the investments were in blue-chip companies: IBM, J.C. Penney, Nordstrom, 3M, Sears, Johnson & Johnson, and FedEx. The list goes on.

"The two things all these companies had in common had been: one, they all had Servant Leaders and, two, they were companies Franklin had either known or talked about. How ironic.

"You see, Mr. Johnson, he never looked at the stock, their prices, or valuation. The dividends that came in he simply reinvested in savings bonds. You received half of his total assets. The balance goes to various charities: MADD, a variety of treatment centers across the country, a men's shelter, and, oh yes, the Humane Society."

"What am I supposed to do with this?"

John grinned like the Chesire Cat. "It's your money to do with as you please. Franklin said you would know what to do." Reaching under his desk, he handed me a box, wrapped with a ribbon. "I'm also supposed to give you this, and wait for you to open it."

The box was enormous. It had an Eddie Bauer logo. I opened it slowly. Inside was a brand new straw hat, a pair of Oshkosh coveralls, and a box of Arturo Fuente Opus X cigars. And there was a note:

Just in case you have decided to make a difference! Love, Franklin.

Epilogue

I eventually sold my company to my employees. It is in good hands. I am now on the road, looking for my first prospect. I know that the Roy Parkers and Ray Fuller Johnsons of this world are out there, and I will find them. I have fully forgiven Parker and myself, too. What a great weight has been lifted off of me. I am free.

I am getting used to these cigars, but for some reason, I can only smoke them with a cup of Starbuck's. Wherever I end up, the town must have a Starbuck's.

I have my resume on the fine parchment paper. I wear the coveralls and the hat with pride. I sold the '52 Ford pickup. Aristotle is fully grown. He is a fine companion.

I still miss my family, but I talk to them each day. I have written many a fine letter to them in my journal. I have read to them aloud many a night. I no longer cry tears of pity and sorrow. Now, my tears are of joy and gratitude. I attend a couple of AA meetings each week. Abundant opportunities to serve await me. Occasionally, I tell a story, mostly about forgiveness and hope. Hope is a great thing, maybe the best of things. But mostly, I just listen, watch, and try to serve others with humility.

I am content. Life is good. Delivering parts is a noble profession, one for which I was born…

Mark Matteson
Mattesonavenue.com
Raising the Bar in Organizations

Mark Matteson is in great demand internationally as a Speaker, Seminar Leader and Consultant. He is the founder and president of Pinnacle Service Group, Inc., Lynnwood, Washington. Mark has been called a Thought Leader, Street Scholar, an Idea Reporter, and an insightful Business Humorist. He is author of three books and four e-books, including the International Best Seller, ***Freedom from Fear***, now translated into Japanese. Mark inspires organizations internationally to **"Raise the Bar"** to achieve higher levels of personal and professional performance.

To contact Mark to deliver a Keynote to your Association or Annual Meeting

Or A Tailored Seminar for your Organization

Or To Sign Up for his Mentoring/Coaching Program

email mark.enjoythejourney.matteson@gmail.com

Voice Mail 877.672.2001 - Cell Phone 206.697.0454

To sign up for Mark's popular monthly e-newletter and receive a Special Report and complimentary e-book go to www.mattesonavenue.com

What People are Saying About
Mark's Seminars

"Great job at our All-Hands Meeting. We did not want you to stop!"
—Kurt Peterson, Microsoft

"The standing ovation and the book signing afterward told me bringing you out was a good investment. Thank you for exceeding my expectations!"
—Rueann Emerson, AFLAC, Lexington, KY

"I have been attending seminars for 20 years. You are the finest speaker I have ever heard.
—David Rhea, Texas Restaurant Association